T0284457

SPRAWL

P

A

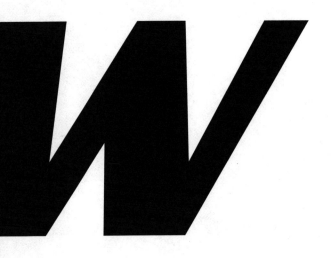

DANIELLE DUTTON

AFTERWORD BY RENEE GLADMAN

WAVE BOOKS

SEATTLE/NEW YORK

Published by Wave Books

www.wavepoetry.com

Copyright © 2010 and 2018 by Danielle Dutton

Afterword copyright © 2018 by Renee Gladman

First Wave Books edition 2018

Wave Books titles are distributed to the trade by

Consortium Book Sales and Distribution

Phone: 800-283-3572 / SAN 631-760x

Library of Congress Cataloging-in-Publication Data

Names: Dutton, Danielle, 1975– author.

Title: Sprawl / Danielle Dutton.

Description: First Wave Books edition. | Seattle ; New York : Wave Books, 2018.

Identifiers: LCCN 2018011301 | ISBN 9781940696775 (trade pbk.)

Subjects: LCSH: Domestic fiction.

Classification: LCC PS3604.U775 S67 2018 | DDC 813/.6—dc23

LC record available at https://lccn.loc.gov/2018011301

SPRAWL was originally published in 2010 by Siglio Press

Designed and composed by Quemadura

Printed in the United States of America

9 8 7 6 5 4 3 2 1

At a certain season of our life we are accustomed

to consider every spot as the possible site of a house.

HENRY DAVID THOREAU

This place is as large as any other town. Each new day there is the coming through of sunlight between the oaks. Things fall and because of this there is a kind of discontinuous innovation. What influences the Richardsons? What influences the Saintsburys? The two questions go hand in hand. How do we cope with the privacy of various domestic characters? The letter, of course, the familiar letter, we employ it. Dear Mrs. Barbauld, It is primarily for the sake of your reorientation to our town that I write to you today. There are more interesting letters, of course. There are no doubt letters with unreserved emotions, just as there are many ways of communicating that are, especially in retrospect, alien to one's own individual experience. It's difficult enough to take in the results, all the sordid aspects. Only gauge what's arisen during old Mr. Anderson's lifetime! The changes have imposed themselves on our features. What does it signify? Flowers, birds, churches, planes, resorts, malls, green places. Industrial clusters and country houses. Today I fell asleep in the tall grass near the old train station. It was a complete picture. A fashionable park. Yet the picture had its sordid and selfish aspect. I can't seem to say what I mean, Mrs. Barbauld, but with some urgency I hope to inform you what a triumph the big city has become. I am a secular individual but even I can feel the shift in the horizon utterly alien to the constitution of things, the habitual. Sincerely, etc. I move in shade on the edge of a parking lot under walnut trees in the early morning around the edge of a curve in an accidental manner. I walk the sidewalk and ripple the surface of it. From this condition I have a view of the world. Magazines provide images of half-cooked food products. Glazed and slick they seduce us like any raw material. Books offer helpful suggestions about how to lead our lives (let the kitchen sparkle, become fully insured, do not approach the side-lines). On the evening news the periphery is always in decline, but we are able to project our own great men into its material present as if extending ourselves into other cultures—an archipelago some-where west of Hawaii (and pineapple rings on grilled hot dogs make "Hilo Franks"). After this we return to normative-centralizing activi-ties, such as the time we made a replica of our town out of sugar cubes, or when we gathered to string garland around every phone booth on Main Street. But Haywood defends himself against my moral intrusions. He stands in the kitchen holding a knife and a mushroom. He says, "Clothe your instructions in less abstract examples." He is angry because he was raised to be a substantial Protestant, with stories of utility to tell the women, and relevance. Without it he gets cranky. I prevail. I appear to be free from design or discretion. It is an easy discovery of the "feminine." I walk through the doorway wearing my aggressively orange hat. I do it over and over. I do it as a kind of series and then I do it in reverse. I do it as an indicator of a particular lifestyle, to redefine myself and exclude others. First I do it in a red pantsuit and then I do it in the nude. I do it and I say, "I doubt it." I twirl a little when I do it. I do it and am striking when I do it because I do it in a frilly dress like meringue. Afterward, we eat bread, corn, cupcakes, cheese, and two chickens, and then we argue about it. We ingest liquids and a bunch of different fruits. Together we forget where we parked the car. We go into houses to witness the presentations. Domestic life appeals to us as well rounded. When we lick each other we do it without any sense of "before" or "nowhere," so you can see we do it as suggested.

Also, we worry for money and are employed worrying about things. While it's been proposed that we are more interesting than characters on television, one day soon we will be characters on television. The story is well told. The water tower can be taken up as a challenge to the mist. It invokes a center relative only to the imperceptible pattern I leave with my footsteps, mostly at night. Feeling like a mist, I look at things, trees. The water tower takes on sonnet form. In my dreams I embellish it with tacky Christmas decorations. I sit at the kitchen counter with the cat by my feet and watch the lights of the city in the distance and a skyscraper. Helicopters and planes revolve around it in peculiar orbit. Meanwhile, the book in my hands says we should try to hone our "sensation of *of, if, the*, and *some* as well as *tree, smoke, shed*, and *road*." I put the book on the counter and go into the yard. I do a little dance somewhere near the fence. I raise my arms above my head and swing my hips. I lower my arms and tap my feet on the grass. I do this for a while, and then I sit on cold lawn furniture, and then I finish cooking dinner. In this place, we eat chicken and peas at least once a week. Once a month we organize three weeks' worth of leftovers and once upon a time Mrs. Richardson introduced a new trend that was spatially interesting; it was intended to embellish our looks like poodle skirts or microwaves. We smoked clove cigarettes and stood in the Millers' backyard. I refer to these as "the early times." And other trends: We wrote poems. I wrote them with Lisle. I wrote her poems and she wrote mine. The subject matter was Egypt. We followed each other around town without looking, like tribal migrations. This was one whole epoch of my life. Later it seemed incomprehensible. Today Haywood uses language to articulate a room and I'm supposed to move inside it. I bump my hips against edges of tabletops, but I'm surprised to find each detail intact and some dramatically more effective than what preceded (two eggs on a white linen tablecloth). It's a kind of new Industrial Age and all our information is encoded or reproduced. I take three or four showers a day, but this would never make it into a biography of the town. What we want is a "true celebrity," an automatic pop star who can supervise the details of our lives. What we lack in inspiration we make up for in public charity, like the time we bought cowboy hats for the nameless kids who wander the town, or the time we all fainted at the murder of Sara Patterson. It's a whole universe of suggestion. There are all sorts of trends in the hedges (pornography, garbage, toxins, booze) and all over the countryside (atomized families, robots, child-rearing, etc.). Mrs. Agnew is vilified for her intake of candy, the unfortunate part she plays in American culture, her red-headed remoteness. I stare at her front yard and try not to be there at all. So I close my eyes and become lightened and shadowed by clouds in the background and the foreground. There are dirty dishes in the sink and blooming roses on the countertop. On the table is a white tablecloth, a honeydew melon, two peaches, a paper napkin, two plates, two spoons, a lollipop. Also there is a ripeness, some strange flavor, erect and curious in my mouth. So I start on foot. For a while I pass nothing but the usual ribbon of lawn, then after a while I pass something else and a dog. Soon I pass Mrs. Clark and Mrs. Aubrey. I say, "This is a really nice lip balm." Then I say, "Set the table," then "Gems!" then "Nope." Later, I ignore myself on purpose, which takes practice. The book in my hands offers an analysis and sometimes a celebration; it says there is an "ascendancy of private, individualized transport." It's true we have ample parking and this is almost impossible to reverse. In the middle of the street are several small household appliances and a round yellow cake, which must have crossed into my path like a glass plate broken in a fit, or a healthy lawn, or a jar of grape jelly at the supermarket. All these things overlap and line up at the same time. I write letters on the white linen tablecloth and the dark blue ink enhances the effect of the cloth by providing stark contrast. Meanwhile, the crows in the yard act like dogs and Mrs. Wick leans over to tell me she's on a journey she likes to call "Mrs. Wick." This gossip involves listening and is for my own good. On the evening news there's a report about a national hero and a story on the two types of food: packaged and unpackaged. I learn there are many methods of preparation, such as freezing, freeze-drying, condensing, and dehydrating. I learn that last year a woman died from tuna fish, which doesn't require mixing or cooking so it's easy for you and your guests. The reporter says top chefs in major cities are using a new type of packaged food; they prepare the food themselves (liver, salmon, ribs, carrots), and seal it in plastic, and freeze it for up to eighteen months. One chef is interviewed. He says the whole world has been cooking the same way for over two hundred years and this has got to change. He shows his tongue to the camera to indicate playfulness and drops a lobster in boiling water. According to the reporter, this gourmet-packaged food can be served at four-star restaurants and to first-class passengers on airplanes and the armed forces defending liberty and freedom in all its forms. So I stand in front of the television holding the remote control. I aim it at myself for what must be twenty years. Then I turn south and take a long walk down sidewalks. There is a range of real activities in this place. One kid says, "Bring me an ice-cream cone," but sometimes you have to read between the lines. There are haircuts and play dates along with corporal punishment, orders, increased comforts, spinning, sleeping, eating, etc. There is love for people named Brittany and people named Jack, and most of us display some skill at pressing faces, or pressing people for infor-mation about what we like and what we find comfortable, or com-forting. For example, we enjoy waterways, car races, immunizations, gymnastics, murals, hamburgers, flowering vines, babysitters, poli-cies and programs, encircling verandas, skateboards, shrubs. Also, we like hoeing and bathing. When he returns from his job in the city, Haywood cleans his ears and asks for a drink. He sits by the fire and talks to the television. He says, "I've been to the outskirts and back again several times." The arrival of cars was one particular epoch in this place. We bought cars whole families could fit in, cars with con-vertible tops, and tin trays for eating, and wonderful colors, and mu-sical horns. Today we have cars with satellite mapping systems and antilock brakes. Also, we have latent perversions and other luxuries and good dinners and youth movements and next year we will not feel more or less crowded or more or less confined than we do tonight. Meanwhile, there is heavenly weather and a letter arrives. Among other things it eloquently and wittily hints at upcoming events. It's a very warm letter, ultra-comfortable. I spend the whole day sitting prominently on the porch, sunbathing in winterish sun, watching a massive and continuous flow of migrating birds. Large birds land on my lawn and flap their wings and shake. I associate myself strongly with them, with the way they put one foot in front of the other, and how they keep their heads aimed at the ground. They eat well. They have a huge and panoramic view of my house, yard, and automobile. We look across the wide green lawn and by the end of the day they've eaten several snails. I make two ribs of beef for dinner, one tuna, four omelets, one iced cucumber soup, two Chinese cabbages, two salads, five hams, one chicken liver, and for dessert I make pears in wine, one strawberry tart, one lemon tart, three apple pies, one bananas foster, and three chocolate cream pies. It's important to consider the effort it takes to survive. The world actually has signs with skulls and crossbones, vermin, separation anxiety, nightmares. But one highly respected tradition in this place is to get away from all that. The organization is based on the theme of American history and has fundamentally changed the feeling of this once-bucolic setting. Nevertheless, everything surprises me, everything I've forgotten, townsmen who belong to me and townsmen who do not, hula hoops, garlic peelers, gulls, sunsets, swimming pools, asphalt, eggs, buttons on the stove, algae, credit cards, crops. I nod and return to my book: "Take any normal street of average length and just consider all that fucking!" Different views: we look at them sideways, up and down roads, transforming trees and boulders into eloquent minilandscapes with subtle lighting and fountains. A kid on the street says, "Rocketry." Another kid says, "Oomph." Then one day there's a broccoli quiche on the edge of my dining room table. It's like a mysterious omen. I'm aroused and I almost lift it up and take it to myself like some seed I'd already planted, but instead I walk around it, all the way around, leaving a crescented track in the carpet with my spike-heeled shoes. Meanwhile, someone is shouting at someone else in Spanish, on the sidewalk, someone in a gray truck. I can't make it out. Dear Mrs. Baxter, Welcome. Your earnest and expensive skepticism is otherworldly. For this reason, I advise you to

take two or three sheets of paper and make a journal of anything remarkable that occurs in the next few days. Idle romances, typo-
graphical reproductions, eye- and ear-witness testimony, the reality
of our special community—I recommend all these pleasures to you
now. You'll need to keep track. You'll have to be strong, Mrs. Baxter.
Everything is different, but over time, to a certain extent, nothing really happens. Such is the critical authenticity of every historical moment. Focus on apprehensible objects and their previously unap-
prehended relationships to other objects around your house or this
place (your body to fish, glass to a quality of mind). It's a deal of fun.
Yours, etc. Noise of a cat running over stiff grass, but the cat doesn't
matter so much as the feelings its tiny feet feel. It bends a sort of
emptiness around. Haywood goes out very naturally and then he
comes back in. He tells people there is such a thing as cultural enchantment. He presents me with all sorts of failed objects. He holds
them up against my body so that I harden into wrinkles and strange
postures. This is in our bedroom or at home in front of a whole shelf
of very terrible books. His arm reaches out and rests on the table and
I hesitate to stand and turn and look. Instead I might function on a
practical level, such as people who hardly ever articulate what they

know, or I might behave in a way to be admired, mounted, like a pretty hen, or a comprehensive weapon to be polished. I stand upright in the garden like a tulip. I stand beside lawn furniture and am more than comfortable. I warm coffee for the chickadees and call them *fellers*. The backyard is thick with blackbirds and squirrels. I walk the whole distance of it. If you go back and forth all day it's like dozens of miles from one end of our house to the neighbor's. Then I go inside and walk past one coffee cup, one spoon, one cherry, eight cherry pits, a half-eaten pear, two paper towels, and a paper napkin on the edge of the dining room table. That afternoon, Haywood plans exacting labors. We close the blinds and in this connection we cannot refute the following statement: "Oh Haywood, Haywood." I bake croutons and stand in the kitchen. Later, I cut across the lawn and run into a dog. Once upon a time this place was home to bears and muskrats, hunters, rum, whip-poor-wills, carts, mud turtles, minks, ducks, loons, donkeys, rabbits, hickories, highway robbery, a stranger with a bun in her hair, and other things you can read about. Today the color blazes, the tulips in the box—violet and vivid green. Our own brand of localism is traced back to settlers of specific persuasion and beautification. These settlers expressed concern for what the book calls "macho sectors of manufacturing," as well as picture windows, pets, churches, bean fields, straight lines, long and shallow rivers, staplers, buffets. For my part, I decide I have the power to influence change in the landscape with remarks, such as: "We're so proud of what we perceive as our heritage." This is the fleeting language of one day. It partakes of parks, hats, stalls, gum. Anyway it's hard to accomplish things that so easily lose their end-in-themselves. It takes so many doors and mouths and stores. The street sings. It might be a mountain of fanned causes, or a hybrid construction, like buildings that shed themselves as they grow, or the weird flavor of onion in your mouth when you start to panic. There never was such a mighty belief system. I dust plants and look out at backyards, at red and green playground equipment, at hot tubs and hoses. For lunch I eat presliced turkey and a disappointingly small piece of avocado. Later, I arrange myself. I decide to take a bath in the middle of the day and stare at myself in the mirror. I observe all kinds of transformations on my skin and in my muscles. I move in different directions, with subtle variations in my eyes or knees, or I crouch by the hamper to play with the cat. Then I fill the tub for goodness knows how long and ornament myself richly with a variety of fragrances. I enjoy raising a bowl of scented water above my head. I sometimes even take an active part in anything strange. The book in my hands describes "a land of enchantment, a garden most gorgeous, a plain sprinkled with coloured meteors, a forest with sparks of purple and ruby and golden fire gemming the foliage." The book says pearls, shells, and certain precious man-made objects can assist in scenarios of craving. I can't wait to open them up to see if there might be something fascinating inside. I do it on a chair or with my hands or feet. I get pleasure from acquiring knowledge about everything from hands and feet to handmade wicker baskets. For instance, the arrangements around the house are meant to show my attention to such items, to things placed at an angle, or pinned up, or to religious teachings (indicated by an open book on a chair), as well as decorations and collections of plates, peaches, candy, etc. Several of my tabletops are tilted for better locating the center of my domestic charisma. It takes approximately three hours to appreciate the importance of a mislaid knife on a wooden table, an enormous stain on a white linen tablecloth, or a landscape of leftovers floating weightless around a room. Meanwhile, a copper pot on its side sends a gleaming reddish glow onto a honeydew melon and a number of household objects: a glass of milk, a bowl with a knife in it, the skin of my own hands. I shift small decorative boxes from room to room and begin to feel ungainly. The small boxes glint in the half-light as I place them in specific patterns, as markers of my own personal history, or like a new museum. In all the boxes are remnants of past relationships, specific locations, like statuettes within homes, or a range of associations—letters, photographs, scraps. Dear Mrs. Roberts, I sympathize with you. I really do. Mrs. Roberts, you possess a kind of impenetrability most Americans find "smart." I feel I *know* you intimately without ever having met you. You are America's Sweetheart. You are like no other person, Mrs. Roberts. You know a lot about how a woman's mind works. Mrs. Roberts, you know just when to start and when to stop. You are seen and heard from south to north. Also, there is a third reason: your house is your castle with its mock-Tudor exterior and precocious children. We all greatly admire your long driveway and eagle ornaments. Warmly, etc. For one whole summer, Lisle and I wore beribboned pigtails and believed the water tower in the center of town was filled with enormous spaghetti and meatballs and that if we were rude or unpleasant a giant meatball would fall out the bottom of the tank and roll down the sidewalks and find us and crush us dead. Years later, Lisle and I applied ourselves sincerely and with tragic dignity to photographs of people long dead, or to stories of mysteries in foreign landscapes, or familiar landscapes, or murder mysteries, or stories of children locked in attics, or cheerleaders, or stickers, or public pageants, or photographs of squirrels, or turtles, or turtles' eggs. For a period we tried to be industrious witches who could open and close doors with our minds. We rode bikes at the edge of town, through orchards and fields, collecting stray cats in baskets. Then Lisle began cutting notches on her ankles or wrists to mark the years. Needless to say, we developed a whole host of human concerns, physical mythologies, and informing personal principles regarding "natural" curls and hair that looks "sexy" or "head-turning," or hair that is "long" and "angled in front for movement." We learned all kinds of protocols involving "how to," such as how to make your life "prettier" or "better organized," or how to get "more bang for your buck," or how to "make a splash," or how to walk through a garden with a rosy bloom on your cheek. These days Haywood and I enjoy walking through the lawn-equipment area in a department store in the mall. There's a smell of chemical fertilizers and a real-life sparrow is trapped in the branches of a potted tree chirping at passing shoppers. In other sectors of the mall we pick out bathroom tile or formal wear or pretzels. We return home and change clothes or put things in cupboards. We hold hands in the dining room. We watch the evening news and learn about competitive ping-pong, hot-air balloons, war, and the latest scandals. Hundreds of people are nominated for awards. We watch the parades on television. Haywood asks, "Whatever happened to real cheese?" We shake boxes of food. This method imposes a deliberation. We postpone dinner and walk the empty street. On the sidewalk I find unfriendly footing on a section turned up by roots, yet leaf-buds delight me. Young boys run by with red fire engines in their arms and complain about the rest of their lives, but looking at the stars I take a cheerful hint and am invaded by the memorable. I whisper to Haywood with a vulgarity that seems surprising. In bed I think of all kinds of individual names, and some numbers, and other names. These aboriginal or primary thoughts are depicted as I drift to sleep. My mind clicks like a machine and I see men walking, and a chair and clock, and a stranger, and a thousand other particular things, and am suddenly bathed in the language of another person, or persons. Then I dream we have an indoor pool and I serve sophisticated snacks to neighbors poolside (tuna tartare and rack of lamb). In the morning, the cat licks Haywood's face before he gets out of bed. It's an approach to nature. Haywood shaves and showers before work. He backs into the street without looking. A husband will do all sorts of things. We stare at each other. Actually, he stands next to me and puts his hand on my shoulder. We are united by all sorts of facts, a divine ordinance, or something like that, slogans. In the pursuit of milk, yogurt, progress, etc., we are long, maybe fourteen feet stretched out, and together we know thousands of miles worth of information. Also, we develop guilt feelings and interpret each other's physical uniformity or discordances; for example, when I see a mysterious spot on his cheek, or when he connects my breathing to what I ate for breakfast (jam on toast and a pot of tea). When we first met I stopped seeing another man so many times a week for so many years in a row. This other man lived in the city and had a habit of forcing his way into my ear, to suck out whatever was in there—air, feelings, space to oneself. This was a last straw. Things were messy. He would be silent because no one would say anything. Maybe he was right. He was certainly enthusiastic and he grabbed my arms and held them over my head when he did it. Today Haywood is tied to the bed and I am going along to vacuum the other room. I shift fruits from the floor to the heavy glass tabletop. I line them up on the edge. It's exciting and I look forward to him telling me how surprising it is to poke and scramble about in the midst of our intimately satisfying personal relationship. On the other hand, less feminine attributes pass through my mind at times like these—everybody's walking barefoot on Mrs. Williams's carpet. They say, "Can you believe it?" We are given fresh glimpses of the ground: mounds of plush gray carpet, pebbles, concrete, trash. No one wants to consider the importance of this earthy destiny. Meanwhile, the kids with no names are all over town. They supply a stylish language with which to talk about serious issues; they live on the edge of my habits. I think I should be allowed to solve their problems. I think about a lot of unnecessary things. For example, I walk down the sidewalk and think about three chairs in my house. Then I get home and observe my dirty floor. A green glass bowl, a peach, a blackberry, an apricot cut in half, cake crumbs, and fallen purple petals litter the tabletop in the kitchen. And yet, in spite of these surroundings, I have friends like everyone else. I have talents and am easily dazzled and I can say "I'm sorry" or "That's the upside" whenever the moment arrives. On any average evening I remove my clothes like anyone else. Afterward, there are a number of erotic rituals. I'm often inaccessible during such amusements. I say stupid things. I say, "Woodpile," or "What's this?" Then I *do* stupid things. There are some misunderstandings and some feathers, and later there is some irritation. Still, I can be anything I set my mind to. I can be a movie-star vixen or a saucy French maid. It's true I turn into a cleaning lady at times. Other times, I refocus my attention on my own movements, such as twisting or turning. I never really meant to be born at such and such a time with such and such habits, but I was raised during the last fifty years and trained to match my outfits to the decor. There are all kinds of chronological stages. For example, there is a parade of lights each year. One townsman tells me it's a time-honored tradition, but I don't believe him. In this place, we once upon a time drank water from leaves and set traps for wolves and North American Indians. We invented houses with conveniences or luxuries or we sat in the open air to gather dust. Travelers passed by in herds, diligently following each other like railroad cars for safety and convenience to saloons run by men with glass eyes. The modern drawing room consisted of a divan, an ottoman, a sunshade, and an oriental rug. Today I imagine busily dusting furniture. Then I imagine throwing furniture out a window instead of dusting it. I imagine dust gathering on broken furniture and horse shit on the ground. Meanwhile, the countertop is crammed with apple and orange peels. A half-eaten lollipop rests on its clear wrapper beside a pestle and mortar, also a white plate dirty from a slice of cherry pie, several aspirin cut into quarters, and an empty glass container. Before lunchtime, alone on the sidewalk, the world rolls by like a magical ride. The ice-cream truck jingles as I pass and all the lawn gnomes offer a cheerful "Hello!" They look out with dead aim at the perfect beauty of lawn care, car pools, mailmen, etc. It's their nature to inhabit such scenes like temple guards. Throughout the day this is more or less the quiet language of the block. It partakes of skinned knees and competes visually with daytime television and advertisements for migraine medication and the sacred rights of citizens. I feel my instincts concentrated in my hands and feet. My feet search out the shallowness of the sidewalk like a clear stream. I follow it by degrees, in soft ripples, around children, churches, lawn mowers, dogs. I don't even think about the permutations of violence or beatitude: plastic marigolds, stone pigs, lawn jockeys. One old man in a blue house in the middle of the block paints his sunflowers red, white, and blue every July. It's my job to send him letters. I ask about the good and the bad. He responds by sending me books on arithmetic or old-time almanacs, but one day he drops dead without having ever entertained me, without ever having written down his wise thoughts, and without actually appearing to know anything beyond his strange whistling to himself and his painted yard. So I have lunch with Mrs. Batt. Together we have long eyelashes and remember many outings and activities, such as being upside down on our heads, or sitting motionless like ducks, as well as ceremonies, disappearances, personal tragedies, and other stories that express whole years, if not centuries. One of the nameless kids who wander the town sits outside the café window drinking coffee from a paper cup. He rocks back and forth, with a sharp jerk at the end of each forward motion, like he's waking himself up one second and falling asleep the next. Up close I can see he has blue eyes and the tips of his fingers are stained from smoking cigarettes. Then I finish my potato salad, as well as a sandwich of tuna fish, mayonnaise, cucumbers, tomatoes, peppers, red onions, and sprouts. The nameless kid talks to himself while I talk to Mrs. Batt. He says, "Scenic vista!" It's true he looks like a climber or adventurer in that coat. Afterward, I take the leftover bread from my sandwich to feed to squirrels and crows in the park. I bend over and roll the bread across the grass. One squirrel runs away from the rolling bread, but the crows don't move at all, but then they do move, toward the bread, sort of nonchalantly. That night I dream I have roots in me and a pot of buried gold, my own buried treasure and I carry it around in my stomach. In the morning I plant petunias and find a marble in the dirt. I chop broccoli at the kitchen counter and with its clean, bitter smell I continue to sharpen and realize. I enjoy the energy the knife gives me, which is somehow constricting and stupid. Later I wash dishes and hum softly and think of old sex-partners, different positions, or beds, how one was just a mattress on the floor and one was in a closet. That one imprinted itself on my memory due to a series of odd gestures involving a sweater and a cock, as well as the calculated intercession of photography. Some photos are destined to be kept in boxes or closed dresser drawers. And some photographs people won't give back even when you ask for them. Still, there are all kinds of pictures displayed on walls and shelves. In some, a family stands with an old man who plays a harp, or there are men wearing hats by bridges, and one indicates harmonious communication between different social classes. There are photos of dogs in wagons, or boys pulling wagons, or stony shores, or boats. In some photographs, whole objects are concealed by other objects, or there are objects partly cut off by a border. At the center of one is a cake on a cake-stand at the edge of a table. On the edge of the countertop, lined up along the edge, is a plastic cutting board with dried tomato pulp, a mixing bowl, a crumpled paper towel, a ramekin, a stack of plates, two tumblers, three spoons, a cold saucepan, a rubber band, a portion of lemon skin, and the cap to a bottle of vinegar. The wallpaper is blue and white. The cat watches me from his central place in the world, with an abstract expression on his mottled face. The following day, Haywood gives me a gift. He puts a ribbon around it, which is loads of fun. It's a gift of pleasure everyone can enjoy. It's a brand-name item, accurately labeled. It could burn two hundred calories per hour and is an object on a string. Afterward, we go to a movie about a beauty and a beast. The girl is blond and a foreigner. She says, "Magnificent," and her eyes shine with tears. But they decide to kill the beast anyway. On the television one senator says he hasn't done anything wrong and then he says he hasn't done anything immoral; they show herds walking in open spaces between banks of snow and then they sing a song about how a bill becomes a law. It's entertaining and has to do with news. In the morning, Haywood reaches for the cereal he wants. I cut a hard-boiled egg. I cut it into two pieces and then I cut it into four pieces. I think about it and then I get a lot of things done. I run my index finger along the rim of a juice glass and stretch my palms on the wooden table. I carefully handle the items on the table: a bowl of grapes, a paper napkin, the wax-paper wrapper to a piece of hard candy (orange), a fork, a spoon, a butter knife embedded in a chocolate muffin dusted with powdered sugar, nine cherry pits, three sesame seeds, a sugared jelly candy (orange), a small shallow bowl painted with flowers, and an oddly shaped rock. There is a larger object on the table just out of reach, which throws its heavy shadow onto my fingers and the napkin. Then Haywood comes home with four kinds of chicken in a bag. He carries a briefcase and the newspaper and rubs his eyes under his glasses. In the *Daily News* they run a column called This Day in History, which does little to bring us nearer the actions of our obsolete settlers. This place has moved ahead, from thing to thing, from crow fences and streets with misspelled foreign names to produce-department decorations and cartoon architecture. We carry large cardboard replicas of asparagus or breakfast cereals. We move on wheels through dusty streets, with hooks, trains, representative politics, satin pajamas, fur coats, deluxe toasters, and an appetite for soap and colonial-style lampposts. We push out, comprising bulk, veins, lanes, migration, and a large selection of signs, or someone pushes in, importing trees and exotic plants. To take advantage of this utopian vision I carefully enjoy the quality of life in neighborhood gardens. I continue walking and pass restaurants and shopping malls, fry pits, carpet warehouses, parking lots, and a mass of yellow traffic signs. I carry a package with twelve subpackages inside it. Each package contains one serving. I am absentminded nearly all the way until I reach the sunny side of my house. It strikes me now that when we wake we often wake unwittingly. I dramatize small moments of my life on the phone or in a public restroom. I am all sorts of things in themselves: I am in character, I am in mint condition, I am in my head, I am in luck, I am in need, I am in vogue, I am in the red, I am in deep, I am in tune, I am in trouble, I am in control, I am in the way. Meanwhile, there are all kinds of decorative details on the buildings downtown, and we hardly know how to explain them. When a traveling show of Dutch paintings comes to the museum in the city (*Market Scene, Fish Market, Market Scene with Ecce Homo, Kitchen Scene, Vegetable and Fruit Market*), Mrs. Bell and I visit it, battling traffic. We pay for our tickets and check our coats at the desk. Then we witness all kinds of narrative illustrations, erotic symbols, vendors and wares, humble objects, peasants bearing trays, and assorted kitchen items, such as marble-topped tables, peeled lemons, grapes. The walls take us through the history of a period and style, in chronological order, with anecdotal and scholarly information in prepaid headsets: "The Bible occupies a dominating position in the center of the table, while the novel is marginally, even precariously, placed on the edge." There is a limp rabbit depicted in shadow on a table beside a plucked chicken. There is a spread of darkness in relation to the white, the light blue, yellow. We interrupt this whole Flemish occasion with trips to the restroom, the reapplication of lipstick, postcards from the gift shop, see-a-drummer-on-a-street-corner, and other sorts of preoccupations (wanton, capricious, assertive, but disorderly, like a body without its head). On the way back to the parking garage I hold my breath when we pass large groups of pedestrians on the street, which is dirty and like a deafening and awful ballet, with people walking into and out of buildings, people carrying purses and shopping bags, people with briefcases and raincoats enjoying undercooked chicken, martinis, cigars. On the drive home Mrs. Bell says, "Everyone can relax." That night I hold my breath underwater in the tub, but I leave my eyes open to observe liquid gel toothpaste, a hair dryer, a plastic hair clip, a gleaming piece of interior decoration, and a custom makeup palette. In the morning, two woodpeckers try to peck their way through the window frame into the kitchen, but the cat lands· on the sill and clucks at them from the back of his throat. This seems unnecessary. But I don't stop the cat because I guess this is his job. That's the quality of one moment; it consists of cruelty, breakfast plates, indecision, a moth-eaten sweater, trees and tulips—tremendously, excitedly, perversely bored—so I turn out my purse on the kitchen table. From the other room the television sounds on without drawing too much attention to itself. My neck hurts. I suppose I need to buy newer and better pillows. But maybe pillows don't have that kind of power after all? Dear Mrs. Henry, Hello. You might wonder at the values and preoccupations ascendant in this region for decades. In particular, Mrs. Henry, allow me to address you on the subject of nice lawns and nice people, hardworking people, neighbors within a neighborhood, people who take care of their own lawns, etc. There are those who believe your front yard is currently implicated in several disruptive notions of "utility, chaos, and a lack of concern for the opinions of others." This is the kind of attitude we prefer be reserved for the backyard. In the front yard, Mrs. Henry, we aim for a distinctly American, park-like, ideological space, a classic composition in which the individual cares for his lawn for the benefit of the connectivity and industriousness of the entire community. Let me suggest that you visualize the lawns on our street as a string of priceless pearls, wherein each pearl is attractive on its own yet indistinguishable from the others. You might as well accept it. This is a major sociological locus for us and one that raises critical questions of beauty and goodness, not only regarding landscaping but also regarding the individual who maintains his lawn as an unquestioned symbol of respect for nice people, or not. Sincerely, etc. I yawn and take a pink sponge from the kitchen to wipe down the dining room table. On the table is a marble cutting board, a paper towel, onion skins, a mango, an empty water glass, a serving spoon, and a reckless spread of crumbs. No doubt someone else might think for me. Someone might at least be possessed with the idea of me. The singing of birds and crickets elevates my dreaming. Haywood's right arm is under my back and his feet hang over the mattress. In the morning he goes out the bedroom door and closes it. Then he goes out the front door. I open windows and doors. I move toward the northernmost wall and open two identical windows. I say, "Meat space," and I move my neck, clockwise, in a careful circle. Of course it's impossible to see the city through the treetops in this haze. I make a pitcher of orange juice and sit. At present, the house is empty. I put on my hat and walk the sidewalk eating a bar of chocolate. From this perspective I see many things that have been thrown away. The most original of these is a composition: radish beside unopened bottle of champagne. Everyone is shocked by the young couple who moved into the two-story house on the corner. It is observed that they are newly arrived from some politically underdeveloped country halfway around the world, some sector in which it is still unsafe to stay overnight, and where there are forts, thoroughfares, and canals, as well as estates, mills, plantations, and meadows. Soon Mrs. Hull reveals that the husband uses bad words and wanders his yard like a lunatic, checking under rocks, plunging into bushes, chasing after birds. I privately consider his behavior as the best way to get to know your yard and grasses. Eventually, the whole town adopts a laissez-faire attitude, and, in the end, the way in which he is absorbed into the visual landscape of the neighborhood is touching and suggestive of regional patriotism. To celebrate, we offer low-interest loans to the nameless kids who wander the town. I am filled to the brim with my own brand of philanthropy and consider writing a speech. Then I eat cheeses and crackers and watch television and eat strawberry preserves on toast. Meanwhile, I hear a variety of sounds that almost take my breath away. I hear someone talking from another yard, making a brutish sound, and loud. But there are stars behind the clouds and a frog beside the pool and really you can't worry too much about all the major things. So I go into the kitchen and stare at the counter. Most of the time I'm pretty much anywhere. I get my hands on tools or strands, or things that pop into my mind like familiar details. I am visually integrated into my domestic background by color, scent, and shape. In some sense I'm madly in love, or I'm transformed into a kind of habitat, or I match the wallpaper with my eyes. It's confusing to have so many plausible alternatives. So I measure our range, our suppleness. Haywood has a different set of commands, which can be alarming and very difficult to pull off. My own instinct is to laugh and yet also to believe it all at the exact same time. Like the way we play in prefabricated social settings. The way we move the furniture around like props and practice entering one room over and over. The way we lick each other, dramatically, framed by the picture window, or how we drop the heavy crimson curtains in front of any outsider's vantage while inside it's still perfectly believable and real: on the evening news a man sits on his couch watching TV, and I sit on my couch, and the interviewer asks the man a question we never hear, and the man says he figures technology will give him a long life even if he just sits there eating. Then Haywood comes in wearing slippers and holding a pear. He places the pear on one corner of the glass-topped coffee table. On another corner is a red apple and in the center is a tangerine. The television cable makes a discrete loop on the carpet. I say, "Synthetic," then "Brisk walk," then "Extract." I offer him food from a package and am confident the package contains the food it claims to. It's true I look stunning in particular colors, such as ivy, peach, and azalea. I rub my nightgown against my breasts and thighs. Dear Mrs. Flick, Welcome. If you don't already know it, you soon will: In this place an alarm clock is going off every minute. People buy this thing or that. People seem to fit into their clothes. If you know anything about it, Mrs. Flick, you'll know that this place has street names like Cherry, Princeton, Sacagawea, and School. It reminds me of paintings of people who sit at Formica-topped tables with crumpled paper napkins and mugs of coffee, or people who sit down to dinners of soup, bread, and wine. Rest assured, I could feed at least twenty people of consequence on the dinners I give. It's a custom here, Mrs. Flick, and there's no use fighting it. I suggest you initiate a period of dinner-making, calmly, for approximately forty years. Yours, etc. It's bewildering, the way faces pass in and out of my line of vision as I sit in the car and wait for the light to turn green. This place tends to take on a benevolent glow when birds peck at the grass in front of the gas station on the corner. I turn left, then right, then left again, right, left, and then I go straight for quite some time, and then I take a right, another left, a right, and then I'm home: driveway, garage, linoleum, a flight of stairs, a river leading west, south, southeast, east. It's so old-fashioned, a memory, unimportant events. Lisle and I once heard a branch fall to the ground. It was a heavy branch, waterlogged and distended. Meanwhile, the oak tree across the street has been there for over a century, since the earliest nostalgic links and sentimental assertions of this place. The roads outside are wet (or the clip-clop of horses' hooves, the bull escaped from the arena up the street and ran downtown during lunch). Haywood takes me to a restaurant for dinner. He encounters new cravings via advertising. The restaurant presents itself as a country kitchen with gingham curtains and blue fires in wood-burning stoves. There is a particular etiquette we observe, which involves particular moments of silence, particular expressions, waving, etc. Back home I shift colorful fruit candies to the dining room table and line them up (yellow, green, orange or orange, green, yellow, red) on the brilliant white tablecloth, which hangs low over the edge to form a sharp contrast with the shadowed wall behind. The arrangement and rearrangement of these everyday objects is comforting and has to do with human nature in the petroleum age. It's a metaphorical tradition involving absentmindedness and materials that do not appear in their natural surroundings, such as strawberries or walnuts, or birds *living* in nests, as well as creative efforts, sequins, and other important leitmotifs. I sort through linen and silver and cookbooks. I find useful instructions for organizing a large banquet, which requires eight courses, a butler, all manner of fruit, cream and cakes, fish served whole, quails and larks, fried venison, pies, cold meat, good soup, bowls with lids, serviettes, saltcellars, and a company of at least thirty illustrious guests. I lift the faucet and get down on my knees and get back up to fill a four-quart pot. Later, I refasten my bra in front of the French doors overlooking the swimming pool and a square of grass. The sun is setting and the sky is arranged in horizontal strips from yellow to blue. In the distance the city flickers. The cat makes crunching noises in some other part of the house. I don't see or hear any birds outside at all. It's a respectable night; I like it well enough. Soon Haywood will have returned from work. His gleaming sedan makes its own cooling noises in the dark garage. The cat goes out the cat-door and then he steps in a hole in the grass and then he turns around and then he repeats this several times. For dinner I make four vegetables and some pork. In the morning I am thick and stiff. I go for a walk and pass cars and SUVs, some with pretty loud music, and then I pass the spot where the meetinghouse burned down. A Chinese restaurant opened there on Easter Day. It opened between a men's apparel store and a stationery store that also sold chairs. It does a rapid lunchtime business and has been here longer than I have with its red wallpaper and jade fish. I continue walking and see the mayor and some hysterical people and some other people who advance on this street between the hours of seven and ten applying tremendous pressure to the asphalt. They may eventually break through and uncover a prior road, a dry road, and you could follow it to the woods in a rapid pace, in a panic, or you could go there slowly, hopefully, with an idea about how you can't stop progress. So I open the door even wider and show them my shoulders or hair. When Haywood gets home I show him my neck, how it rises out of my dress, and how even my new necklace bumps against it. He has to stop and think about that. He says, "Dear," and fingers the beads without looking at them. I serve him from the left-hand side. I serve steak with mashed potatoes and salad, and then I serve several prepackaged puddings. When I remove the plates I do it from the right. I shake myself when this is done. I shake from head to foot like a duck. I shake in lavender ruffles that frame my face. It's important to realize that I shake like a piper-grass in the woods. I shake near the kitchen and then I shake by the bathroom door. When I shake I am dainty and tranquil. I shake without sentiment or doubt. I shake and am somewhat disconcerting when I shake be-cause I shake for ten or fifteen years. Then I scent myself with leftover lemon slices. I stand in the kitchen and look out at the yard. Giant blackbirds take over the front yard. They take over the backyard and exist like obvious symbols on the picnic table. They situate themselves for purposes of leisure, or for purposes of establishing positions and seats of power. Haywood says, "Wake up," as a glass plate of pickles tumbles from the table to the floor. Then a letter arrives, which indicates that Mrs. Nelson will host a party where members of her family will perform their talents, but on the way there Haywood and I get sidetracked, from street to street. We are eager to. We stop the car and move to a bench in the park. We carry on. After this I acquire a faint blush, like a cunning sportsman. I pile flowers on my head. Haywood touches me to indicate he admires and is entertained by my pleasing form. It's true he is entertained by it. So I travel around in the fragrance of a very hazy day. I walk the sidewalk passing garbage cans and dogs and fresh plots of dirt. Then I return home to toasted oats on the kitchen counter, a crystal vase with dirty water and fading flower stems, fallen petals, fallen pistils, a blue-and-white plate, a blue-and-white creamer, two yellow cherry tomatoes, and a glass pitcher of juice. I stand up. I yell, "Pluck!" I yell at the cat through an open window as he tears across the yard chasing squirrels. My affection for the squirrels was born years ago in a grove of elms on the edge of town. The smallest squirrel in the world followed me down a short section of path and stood on my shoe. Today Haywood carries several dried cereals in individual serving packets—an indicator of the vast machinery of breakfast. Each box is lined with waterproof waxed paper so he can eat breakfast out of the box on the way to work. Meanwhile, through elaborate codes and verbal specifications, I articulate as precisely as possible that the fruit I have bought is eternally ripe and high in other benefits for the eater (purple grapes, green apples, red apples). One kid says, "Add more water." Another kid says, "Bombs away." The next day, I carry a piece of fruit to a woman on a bench beside a dog. We eat macaroni salad and remember all the things we've ever said. We talk about what other people have said, and then we talk about particular people, and other people, and people we remember and what they do. Haywood is laughing. He never rises so high as when neighborhood ladies worship his passionless form of beauty (cocktail onions, three glasses, ice cubes). In the late afternoon, men present or absent themselves. The circumstances vary to fit different customs or hours. One man might be in a house, while one might not be there for fifty years. One man might look at two women in one house, and another man might walk into a room and explode. We apologize to each other and affirm it with something that resembles dancing. Then the smells in the neighborhood reach a peak of perfection: meat and sauces, fresh-cut grasses, hotdogs and stacks of pancakes. The book in my hands says, "They did not look like conquerors." Simultaneously, there are other enhancements for domestic weekends, for male and female adults, for predominately male experiences, for homey environments and moments involving mirrors and track lighting and glances that "flirt," or glances that "convey anger" or a "spatial sense of time." Seen from above, there's an attractive pattern to our expansion. The streets form a kind of social meditation, with cul-de-sacs for emphasis, for music and drama. We have a distinctive ecology involving cows, furniture, farms, real estate, azaleas, fires, corn, curtains, dust, passion, malefactors, milk, meat, cherries, wasps, mayors, pipe fitters, fences. Still, the city resists and defines us. It's like one of the last legends, a ritual casting off, a sloughing. A highway connects us to the northwestern edge-towns— forcefully and swiftly, it turns out. So we sit on the couch and drink cocktails with umbrellas and are strongly on this one side of taxation, with an emphasis on judges, unpleasant violent crime, serenity, the good life, biographies of famous leaders, science fiction, and marijuana. I say, "Thanks for coming." Then I say, "Sakes alive!" Meanwhile, the cat tolerates my presence in his tiny sphere of physicality and the microwave disturbs all convention. I live dangerously; I stand in front of the microwave and stare at food revolving. It's harder to stand still than to tell a story. But by effacing all other operations I may come to something important, standing here. Haywood passes me on his way to the garage. I hear the door close and watch his car move down the street. A lot of these dilemmas aren't ever solved. They're like rotting fruit concealed beneath their own sweet smell. I wander around an array of objects meant to convey luxury and plentitude. This is further emphasized by Haywood's new beard, which is representative of a lost tradition of safety and justice. Meanwhile, the cat spends the whole day trying to find the perfect place to sit down. He is shiny and metallic gray. Also he opens up with brownish patches near the bottom, like a fan. He hunts in backyard gardens and brings home clicking insects or birds. He arranges these various prizes half-alive in glorified transpositions of hunting scenes, which are mainly documentary in character.

This makes him a poacher and also indicates how he is driven by hunger and want. On the sideboard: a mysterious orange stain, a blue dishtowel, a silver tray under an empty glass, a wilted piece of lettuce, the top to a bottle of seltzer, a small silver bowl with its silver spoon, cracker crumbs, a tiny fleck of relish. At some point, Haywood writes a check with no real desire to buy anything. We read the check over and over. In the meantime, on the lawn across the street, bronze chipmunks chew small bronze nuts. You could reach out to touch them from the black-and-white striped furniture, which is the other aesthetic object in this picture of a front yard. In the middle of the street, facing east, I am fascinated by performances in front of the PlayStation in the house next door. Voices emerge from an open window: intergalactic space stations, plumbers, child trouble, cancer, belching, etc. In the springtime it's like this. Suddenly we know we will survive. The whole street gathers together in self-inflicted ecstasy, in the Richardsons' backyard. Mrs. Moody wriggles alone by the swimming pool, which is covered in tight blue plastic. Some strange newcomer hands me a beer. He looks at me and then he makes an alteration and then a car pulls into the driveway, which is distracting. Later I watch as he communicates himself to others—he opens the back door and stands outside it with Mrs. Donovan. It's a noticeable shift from winter's operatic melodrama. We sit on blankets and contemplate grass, mouths, mouths, cotton brassieres, relish. I could do all sorts of things. I stare at a blank vertical wall, sometimes, a real wall, which builds a proximal space. Or else I register the elongated flappiness of the body, or long-necked pitchers, or a thumb pinching off clay. On the edge of the table, a jar, its strange softness, the way it records light and the action of hands on fruit and other surrounding artifacts. There is an alteration of bright yellow and bright green on the insides of my eyelids when I imagine a spatial value of nearness. Haywood stands at forty-five degrees and runs his hand through his hair. He is, at times, disinclined to be visible. He gets into bed and presses my leg under the sheets. There is a burnishing, a tactile space for rubbing, which is strangely motionless at some times of the year. Other times there's a real positive self-help philosophy and we partake of it. The division of labor is clear. Maybe I fool around with singing or with having *beautiful* nails or just walking down the street. Maybe I'm possessed by some new ideal, to preserve historical patterns and boundaries, or be merely decorative. For example, there's a new addiction local women negotiate in different ways, on separate blocks, in pantsuits and bathrobes, in houses and public spaces. It's concealed between stones and transferred from neighbor to neighbor via gossip. I involve myself in it like anyone else. Or maybe I just think about it. Anyway, the book says lemon and orange juices have medicinal properties. It shows sweet and sour citrus fruits together on one page. Other fruit is admired for its geometrical construction (apple, melon, cucumber, etc.). I am completely interested in plates of fruit, or fruit baskets, or baskets of fruits and flowers. I have theories of arrangement I share with Mrs. Way and Mrs. Daniels when they arrive. I set out one basket of peaches and grapes, and then I set out a plate with peaches, grapes, apricots, and roses. In the window facing the street is a large vase of flowers (carnations, irises, tulips, bluebells), and one seashell, and a bowl of candy, and a cricket. These displays are in a state of perpetual readiness. Moonlight pours in the open window. The mixture of consumerism and eroticism is particularly commented on. For dessert I serve cherries and strawberries in dark china bowls on a white tablecloth with hard precision. They fight for them like animals. Meanwhile, Haywood and the other husbands eat "normal" bread and place the mustard front and center. I walk outside different conversations. I make my way into the background like a chorus girl or serving wench. I do it on purpose *and* by accident. All sorts of men look at me as I move in confined spaces, with a few tears, or while I exercise. I sidestep very interesting eye contact, but on the drive home I rejoice that there are frogs croaking unseen in the grass. I lay my hands on the steering wheel and admire my painted nails, which are waterproof and a new kind of color with a strange sort of name beginning *gl* (reminiscent of lichen and bird eggs). On the evening news someone is always shocked about public masturbation. I can think of five hundred reasons for such behavior. It depends on what sort of effect you're going for, whether you want to be ignored or avoided for some particular reason having to do with taste or decorum or for any other reason you can think of. I stand in the kitchen holding a glass of iced tea. I say, "Golly." I kick a junk-food habit and don't go overboard with it. I buy the basics. It's like a long, overdue siesta. But later that night there are great productions of metaphors when Haywood returns from the city. He tells me Hannah Green rumbles through his mind like a gilded spirit. This lady, how far could I throw her? What particular words could I throw down at her feet? I style my hair before every disjointed outburst I unleash. I say, "Stand aside!" then "Fuck you!" then "Per-petuation!" I spend a quarter of an hour offering my own take on harmony and consensus in a homogenous society. Haywood pours a glass of milk. Then I take hold of a pile of decomposing vegetable matter and superimpose it on the kitchen floor. I punctuate all this with italics, with large letters. It's important to realize how soft my hair is, how it shines when I bend over the news. He returns days later. I wear a light orange coat and stand in the garden. I am not with-out certainty at his offense. He sleeps in the guestroom, which is just like a sitcom. I sleep in silk, my mind doodling on the pillow as I go. Then I buy rosemary at the nursery near the Church of the Naza-rene and plant it in the front yard beside the illusion of a brook. The impression I retain is that all this is necessary for the development of certain internal inflections and rhythms. Over dinner he says, "We should surrender ourselves completely and for psychological reasons." This is fine. He exemplifies his social group. It is appro-priate. We will find something to hold on to in our pockets or under our pillows. When we lick each other it will be without concern for an outcome of possible delirium or a jumbled pile of want. It will be merely an extension or confession of necessary life. Yet despite our muscular physiques we are possibly even flatter than the previous generation, casting shadows on walls while playing with a kiwi skin or the tab from a can of soda. I can't decide whether my shadow is on the wall or glued to the wall. I'm almost stripped of emotional weight. Therefore, I'm a model vision. I fawn over objects around the room: silver, glass, mother-o'-pearl, fish, fabric, fruit, and so on. I put my hands on shadows on walls. Life suddenly seems more painterly than ever before. I'm half afraid. Tulips stand straight up from the ground like an army, pink and suddenly transformed. The carpet moves like rain. A dim window is full of meaning. An empty transparence of decaying life is like a whole new theory of the universe (on branches, grass, countertops), or a wide circle of waiting patiently, arranging. I am seized by flowers, pink ones. I do the laundry and eat scrambled eggs. I sit alone like a shape on the couch. I miss the point entirely, and this is fantastic. Later, I walk along the sidewalk under a bird in flight, which is a large bird, heavy and dawdling. In this place, we've constructed walls and other fixtures, such as faucets that drip, or disproportionately large decorations for doorbells or toilet paper. I drink coffee with the cat on my lap and write imaginary letters to the strange newcomer about unrestrained gluttony, spiritual well-being, tied-up purses, and other things: games of cards, collections, tides. Another of my attributes is that I love to smell the bud of my own rose. One kid says, "That's not my name." Another kid says, "Quack-quack." Meanwhile, the cat clacks his jaws as he sleeps and Haywood isn't home. I take a walk in the middle of the night. I put on a skirt, a sweater, and a pair of running shoes. I walk the concrete in a performance to be broadcast live. I walk the sidewalks for inclusion into furnished apartments like boxes of plastic marigolds. The darkness participates in my near-sightedness in interesting ways. It depersonalizes things and little strips of time. I aim metaphorically in one direction but wind up on the opposite side of a parking lot. Individually owned plots of land sparkle in the starlight, with pots of soup, sleeping pills, machines, blossoming, the synergism of proliferation, the contemporary lawn, the mown lawn, the smooth lawn, the velvet carpet (replacing the rough meadow). In the moonlight I find a pair of flip-flops, a bag of chips, a gold-foil wrapper, an old knife, a fork, a dead bee, paper towels, a plastic cutting board, and a pile of rotting apples—and I imagine I observe the Sea of Tranquillity with my bare eyes. But halfway through the morning news they show a fox trapped on a grassy median of the highway. So I get back in bed. I play solitaire. I listen to folk songs and file my nails and finish off last night's meat loaf. One of my favorite leisure activities is to gaze at the gate. I estimate that twelve thousand people have passed through it. I break them into categories based on lines of race, class, and creed. They come from airport lounges, malls, and high-tech urban environments. This, in turn, heightens my sense of civic involvement. Maybe I'll run for mayor and theorize relations between gated communities, their political or jurisdictional construct, or the way you can *sit* in them all afternoon. It has to do with obsolete social traditions, the "friendliest towns in America," and studies performed in what the book calls "residential or social enclaves." It's part of a crucial project for expanding cities, semirural zones, and nurturing desirable, straight, regular spaces—houses with space on all sides. For now, rows of lavender and other lawnscaping features have firsthand knowledge of the most highly significant private worlds of the family. There's a kind of sprightly gayness expressed on the sidewalk between bushes, from bush to bush. "Would you like a sandwich?" one person asks. This place is not a ghost town; mothers, businessmen, bus drivers, all sorts of people dream at night in the spaces between driveways, the houses between rows of bushes, all at the same time, dreaming about girl cousins and guns, sailing and London broil, and sprinklers ticking, and hidden cameras, and panoramas, and axes. In the morning, we eat breakfast beside a small green vase bursting with orange petals. On the other side of the sliding-glass door is a flagstone path leading to a pretty walk between ferns. There are strawberry stems on the tablecloth, several juice glasses, a half-eaten bran muffin, a pink napkin, a net. There are crumbs and stains, and the morning light devours what it sees. I take a walk in the garden, which is just like the countryside. I write letters to people elsewhere in America, idealizing simple faith, fidelity, and pastoral elements from the past. Then I look out for woodchucks. I sit behind a door in my house with a jacket around my shoulders and think about a collapsing consecutiveness. Another day I have especially sexual wants. Hate and fear rise out of the metropolis; I glimpse it from my bathroom window when the wind blows the trees just right. These are the feverish excitements of the place. We identify with metaphors about need and space. It is central to our values, which range from sexual depravity to temperance to melodrama. Then, in the middle of the afternoon, someone sends a rake against the asphalt. I grab my hat, full of enthusiasm, and head outside to seek kinship with others, but the street is deserted. Instead, I continue to function alone in the house. I am essentially productive and genuine and important. I bake banana bread and paint the ceiling. On the TV is an interview with a young woman saying loudly, "Could I? Could I?" Later, a little boy in a driveway tells me he has three superpowers: eating yogurt with his eyes closed, reading upside down, and breathing warm air. A smaller boy drops a plastic gun and runs over to say: "Even my superpower is jumping on one foot." But anybody can do that. So I jump on one foot for fifteen years, and he jumps too, and the other boy watches blandly from the seat of his bike, and no one walks down the sidewalk or drives down the street at all. I might as well think of this as the period of jumping. Once upon a time there was a whole period when housewives were dying. Sons came home and found their mothers facedown and blue on the kitchen table. Later there was an era of divorce. This coincided with an upsurge in the popularity of crockpots. Today multicolored pinwheels blow on a lawn, also holiday bouquets and sparklers, also flags, and there is a mailbox shaped like a giant trout. Mrs. Lancing tells me when she moved in there was just a field behind her house. "But you'll get used to anything," she says. Then one day the sun is so bright I have to close all the blinds and curtains. This is an incessant labor with my hands. The sun makes research impossible. I leave the morning paper and whatever books or cookbooks and go outside to hoe beans in my fashionable kitchen garden. On TV I learn the French word for this is *potager.* Over fences I see other women hoeing beans without danger or dissipation in their own well-appointed backyards, and one woman is floating on water with a wrinkled infant in her arms. Some of the women stand upright and look me straight in the eye, and other women are hardly visible anywhere. Some women wave and some women go inside and other women show solidarity with casseroles or pies. Later in the day, I set out to place coffee cups in peculiar positions, and then to combine myself, in slow fashion, with objects that are off balance. I stand on the edge of the dining room table, all bathed in light, for nearly twenty minutes, which seems to freeze time. I balance nectarines on my arms and head, as well as mildewed peaches, which have not lost their fresh scent. I combine oatmeal and honey and slather it on my thighs to firm skin. I move backward as I set the table for dinner. I place dishes upside down on top of glasses and frost a cake and place it upside down on a plate. In this way, I am able to create a disorder on the table that measures routine gestures and the utilization of routine gestures. It's a subtle gradation. When Haywood gets home I present him with a spectacular feast, rich in color and juices. All the plates are right-side up, and, in general, the objects that were off balance are back on. Meanwhile, Mrs. McGowan and Mrs. Pater are very dense and quite beautiful. One works in a pet shop and the other has a husband who is a dentist. The only rule is to say "Thank God!" whenever you wake up in the morning, first thing in the morning, or when you make lists, or just whenever. For a change, I take Mrs. Hudson to lunch. She tells me cheese gives her loose bowels. Then I talk to one family member on the phone for what must be half my life. For dessert I have two scoops of mint-flavored ice cream and then I listen to a talk-show host who asks uncomfortable questions about germs, pants, finger-fucking, etc. Haywood has concerns about getting older and plays racquetball in the city several times a week. At night we are often stirred by the show of light and color. Meanwhile, there is a burning smell. When the telephone rings I have a flight-or-fight response, so I turn off the ringer on all the phones except one in the kitchen and one in the bedroom, and on those two I turn the volume down and change the ring from a ring to a song. Delightful! And now when someone calls the house is filled with a quiet tinkling and I'm pleased as punch to answer and have flexible and fluid conversations with salesmen, policemen, firemen, etc. The next day, Haywood spends time in the city creating wealth. In the long run, men "work" on the weekend, but there are other enhancements, a way to push a little further. I put on my hat and swing my arms when I walk. I get a space-age makeover at the salon on Main Street. It's like I'm the first woman to visit the moon! I've been invited to the space lab and I wonder what to wear. I walk furiously, swinging my arms, but it becomes clear that space helmets were not fashioned for everyday life. Still, I let myself be carried along for the whole afternoon. My feet hit the sidewalk like the shallow bottom of a river. I pass parking lots, car lots, exits, and entrances. People stare at me from vehicles with sidelong glances. I don't let myself get lost. I follow Golden Oldies to a gas station and go inside to drink red fruit punch through a plastic straw. It's a whole imperfect solution to perverse social relationships, single girls and liberated young women, private fantasies, orange-juice substitute, the bumpy horizon. I say, "I am very familiar with your happy expressions." I say, "Wrong answer," then "Pepper," then "Debt." Nevertheless, suburban domesticity continues to throb in the night, despite unflattering photographs of Mrs. Wylie and Mrs. Williams. In the morning, I notice a smear on one of the window-panes. There are crickets in the yard and later I plant a tree. It's a fait accompli. It's in front of the picture window. Next spring it'll be a whole picture of cherry-colored blossoms meant to match the crimson curtains in the front room. It satisfies the tastes of nature lovers and is indicative of annexed growth. It's impossible to say if it will be successful. It's a large painting of a tree on canvas, with a refrigerator in the background, and an American home with electricity wires and other wires leading to the house next door. This is part of the setting in which my body moves, up and down, on furniture and onto the floor, naked or pissing, with food and separate tools. When garbage trucks first became mechanized, Lisle and I would wake early to watch the big metal arm reach out and grab the can and lurch. Today I direct conversation toward other concerns. Haywood thinks about the things we should use. He stands in a contemporary style, next to rattan furniture. He jumps up and down in the backyard and waves his arms for circulation. He washes his face every time he passes a sink. He answers his mail. He is embodied by choices and will never, never, never use himself up. He says, "Put away your precious lingerie." This is where I draw the line. I campaign hard with cheese-and-pimiento sandwiches. I rub myself against him and slip covers over the furniture. I offer a wide range of complimentary gifts, such as beautiful colors, crackers, trembling soap bubbles, the hollow of my neck or back. But everything has two sides and sometimes a variety of others. I flip over like a hundred thousand fish; I am transfixed by his uncanny way of seeing; I am transparent like a membrane, or like a building made of glass with the gates left open. Still, each day is touched by loving lists of mundane objects. I make all sorts of ordinary choices. These are very real and are made up of realistic representations of food, price-cutting, and other traditions. I usually select them for consumption based on investigations into different systems of digestion, as well as preoccupations with myself and the group. Note the compromises I make regarding neighbors' dogs and children, kitchen pieces, small trays with fruit, etc. Grilling is one venerable tradition in this place, not only among men, but mostly among suburban, white, middle-class men with aprons. It's a kind of artistic expression involving propane, meat, large-scale lawn equipment, pools, and fences. I vegetate and dissipate and sit in the backyard reading. For my part, I think people should stare at each other with saucerlike eyes and curiosity. I wear sunglasses and wrap a blanket around my feet. Haywood is howling with laughter in front of the driveway. He loves to shine during any festival. Small birds rush out of the branches while neighborhood women cook up endearing names for themselves or their unruly children. Meanwhile, the book in my hands says, "The air is full of invisible bolts." I wrap the blanket over my head and shoulders. I pretend to be a European actress with éclat and at least a dozen interesting movies to her name. That night Haywood disappears for what seems like two days. The next morning I don't know where to find anything. My stomach hurts and I project sympathy onto myself and then all of a sudden I panic about losing things. I water plants and sit down for more than six hours sorting and sorting. I read through long wild letters, scented. There are shorter letters, letters sent from room to room, letters like sudden flashes, like ferns, gibes, flings, ways ("this land is your land, this land is my land"). I walk from room to room tying down facts and bits of paper. I eat hard candy on my hands and knees. Dear Mrs. Leslie, Take heed.

Certain people have become married, certain streets have become diversified, certain birds continue to peck, and certain lines have been drawn in certain proverbial sands. I could, of course, reduce the number of utensils in my kitchen if I wanted to. I could endear myself to people with certain words or looks. I could become confused with a particular kind of behavior, or I could confuse others with my particularly confusing conduct. Why do I address myself to you at all? Is it to force a sort of careful trotting out of days, weeks, months, and years? Is it to celebrate your several guest appearances at the supermarket or in my driveway? Or is it to remind us both, Mrs. Leslie, that black events will eventually fade and disappear, or that black events will never fade and never disappear? Be honest, Mrs. Leslie, will the best letters of our lifetime be published, or will we store them in pretty boxes, in cool cellars, even the ones I especially like to read, as proof of the power of our ambition, our uncollaborative dedication? Will you dust them at Easter, at Halloween? How long will you continue to go down there at all? Sincerely, etc. I insist on being taken seriously by all the birds in the gaps in the branches of all my trees. I go outside and have a fake picnic. I scrub things and feminize and sexualize myself. Haywood gets home and the expression in my eyes is recognizable from recent magazine covers. I'm so aroused I might rub myself against the new electric gate. Haywood gorges himself on small cakes, some with pink frosting and silver balls, some with greenish fondant and chocolate stripes. For days, paper doilies littered with stale crumbs linger on end tables and countertops. There are all kinds of oppressive principles in the roses and rhododendrons. You can't always find them in the dark. You have to look and look. These problems provide a variety of challenges: voyeurs, traffic violations, hassles with real-estate agents, pining for the past, and other things about which the book "recommendeth men to the favour of women and strangers." Mostly it has to do with outdated notions of wholesomeness. I ask blank questions in the presence of dogs. I stand on a spot in the park and sound great. I say, "Teeth," and "Webbed feet," and "Rock formation." Then I say totally different things, and then the exact same things over and over for what must be a thousand years. Afterward, I examine a coffee-table book of the earth as seen from the air. On the television is a movie about a dream house that awakens unusual longings in a young man with a simple hairstyle. A plastic blue bowl, two slices of pizza, and two paper napkins are arranged on the kitchen counter. The next day we have "Aloha Burgers" in the food court. We sit in traffic and watch sunlight reflect off the mirrored sides of office buildings. On the car radio a state representative apologizes for recent behavior. Carbon monoxide and ozone are no longer subjects of debate. We are destined to destroy a world characterized by the unrefined. It makes an uneasy, ironic consumption. In turn, I prepare an honest dinner, reassuring in all its surfaces. I run my toe up the side of Haywood's socks. I lay my hand on the butter dish. The sugar bowl with blue lace patterns sits at the edge of the table. It might even hover centimeters above the linen tablecloth. A saucer has pink, yellow, and blue flowers, a gold rim. Two blue candles, half melted, stand at odd angles in mismatched brass candlesticks—it is the one family heirloom in this picture of private spaces. The bedroom is a whole other question of a public kind of dreaming, with a different set of buttons, different catalogues, etc. At night I imagine every person in town reading letters in carpeted bedrooms, letters that offer glimpses of other bedrooms, of country-music bedrooms, or sadomasochistic bedrooms, movie-star bedrooms, singer-songwriter bedrooms, the bedrooms of enemies or neighbors, of wealthy Americans, serious or well-designed bedrooms, bedrooms in blue houses or beige ones. I myself admire passionately and with fetishistic interest the bedrooms in high-value land sites. Our own bedroom boasts silky-smooth sheets and creamy colors. It started with embroidered pillowcases and thread counts of 250 or higher, to which I added goose-down-and-feather-fill, an innerspring mattress, and hues that harmonize with my eyes and skin. I stand in the bedroom and I am the thing peculiar in it. I watch myself in the mirrored closet doors. I can't take my eyes off myself. I wear high-heeled shoes and a pinstriped bra. I have a glass in my hand and a satin ribbon in my hair. I am off balance and show signs of recent handling. Then I invigorate it all with a dash of white and lots of chartreuse and a plush throw in velvet. There is a massive stain on a white cloth. I say, "Put the photos in an album," and "Put your back against the wall." But this is disproportionate. There have been complaints. Dear Mrs. Millet, This may seem a bit extreme. It may take more of your time than was previously calculated. No doubt it means different things to different people, different things to people in front- and backyards, people with good lawns and bad, people in danger and people in swimming pools. It deals almost exclusively with barbaric self-indulgence. I have only the best intentions. Mrs. Millet, it's time you adopt a practical approach to native plants, to the aesthetic and financial requirements of residential land use, to cutting down that spruce tree and considering the greater public good. I mean to be frank, Mrs. Millet. There is danger of complete degeneration. Aren't you concerned? Don't you want to know the answer? Don't you want to feel it warming your skin and hands? Mrs. Millet, you must give notice to things used and owned. This is not a "natural" state of affairs. Kill your pests and weeds. Sincerely, etc. In the morning, on the countertop, there's a plate smeared with yolk, evidence of cheese, an olive pit, two butcher knives, a wooden cutting board, a metal strainer, a wooden spoon, a Tupperware lid, a piece of bread, and a Chinese bowl filled with lemons. I see a dead dog on the side of the road and get home to consider a life bare of creature comforts, or a life filled with oral ballads, or the marked patterns of quilts. Gathered together on one small section of the kitchen table is a stack of bills, a plate with the shell of a hard-boiled egg, orange peels, two glasses, one linen napkin, one spoon, and near the edge is an empty box of chocolates (gold foil). In the evening I go for a walk through proposed developments that mean different things to different people and I remember late one night I genuinely desired to talk with Lisle. I got out of bed in my night-gown and walked down the street to her house and up the path and knocked on the large front door. Someone must have had to get up in the dark and slip down the stairs to open it. I think about my own home as an auspicious site for an increase in population and economy. When my doorbell rings I step onto the welcome mat, but no one's there. I'm confronted with a kind of information over-load, the constant noise—the doorbells, lawn mowers, leaf blowers, car horns, babies, grocery carts, electric dog collars, electric gates, mousetraps, garage doors, television aerials squeaking in the breeze, decorative weather vanes squeaking in the breeze, car doors, doors slamming, satellites, airplanes, bouncing balls, and the electric gui-tar of the teenage boy next door. I sit in an upstairs bedroom and comfort myself with boredom. In the afternoon, there's a picnic be-neath the water tower. Carnal motives are signaled by the position of clothing, hats, flowers, the way the interplay of floral patterns, polka dots, and silk scarves hide wifely sorrows. Next to the Old Red Barn, where we sell fudge to tourists, teenagers push against each other. It is not a vague scene. The unfolding friction of their lives draws attention to itself like a movie camera. I can't take my eyes from it. Compared to this, daytime television fails me. These are warm scenes, in the presence of neighbors. The summer is upon us as a kind of kidnapping. Afterward, I hear they wonder if they were ill, walking with carnations in their hair, with sheer lips, that kind of talk. I stand in the Richardsons' swimming pool up to my middle. Mrs. Richardson raises a glass. Mr. Richardson grills burgers on the lawn. Haywood flirts with Mrs. Bonn and Mrs. Odol under a fruit tree. Small birds twitter around a piece of cheese under a plastic chair, and I catch the eye of the strange newcomer who eats guacamole with Mrs. Robin and her daughter and who looks attractive with his legs stretched out on the grass. Alone in the pool I touch my bent elbows to the surface of the water; I break the surface with them. I survey the yard on all sides. Then I do girlish things in the pool, such as laughing, splashing, and enjoying a glass of sparkling wine. I sit on the warm concrete and leave a wet mark and bits of bean pods, tomatoes, and plums. Finally, I make haste to escape the rain, which is suddenly, steadily falling. Wearing only my bathing suit and my glistening orange hat I stalk through neighbors' lawns, picking flowers and knowing it. One man and one wife and several children probably observe this strange phenomenon. I hear doors and windows slamming as I go. I hear the evening news through screened-in porches. When I get home, Haywood isn't there. I say, "Stick a fork in it." I hang my wet swimsuit on the back door and crawl right into bed. I have a terrible dream when the thunder begins during the night. It's terrible enough to base a whole superstition on it. Then in the morning Haywood and I shop for brand-name labeling and other wrappings and packages. On the way home we see a double rainbow stretching over the wet streets and houses (red, orange, yellow, green, blue, indigo, violet, red, orange, yellow, green, blue, indigo, violet). I want to say something. I listen, but there's no sound at all. The dark clouds, how they hang against the sky! For dinner we have hot dogs and beer. It's a cool night. The neighbor's dog keeps barking in the hedge. "Are you ready?" I finally ask. But he just keeps snuffling the grass like an instinct. "Keep it up," I reply, very specifically. Then Haywood beguiles me with something like eternal freshness (a glass of water and orange wedges on a green glass plate); he pursues me in this manner. He smiles broadly and stands in a clean white shirt. He says, "Slow down," and "Right there." Roughly twenty minutes later, my elegant mess, my smell of powder and skin—one might not think it, but the difference in the images, the hue, the pace from one end of the room to the other reverberates in my feet, down into my half-sleep, dancing before me in the name of "what *is* out there" and other things. I never tire of them. I mess it up for its own sake to watch it rotting, in peculiar positions, asleep on a high mountaintop or mildewing in the sink. Afterward, it's easy to recognize. Just look at the way he picks me up and puts me back down. The next day, my horoscope says a relationship will shift for better or worse. Get ready, it says. It says I should take the first step to watch my own dreams become a reality. It says a stranger could play an important part. It says I'm almost already there. It says I should take care of my health. Then it says I should demand straight answers. It says something confusing about a black hole. It says, "Bring together a colorful assortment of guests." It says I shouldn't leave the house. Then it says I'm operating at 1,000 percent. I must take advantage of this opportunity. I must sparkle. It says, "Bling!" It says love is a complete mystery but good friends tell the truth. Travel might be part of the plan, and a new moon in my ninth house, and a cosmetic treatment, or a socially active season, or a midmonth cold. I might be a money-magnet if I'd let down my defenses. It says TLC. I learn the strange newcomer can have an icy demeanor. The horoscope suggests he might be burning the candle at both ends. He might be craving mental stimulation. He might be on the skids. Thanks to a friendly moon it says I could hold the key to a whole planet of happiness. He has a bronzed neck and a hometown but really everyone is welcome in our intimate system. I admire him from several perspectives. Mrs. Zane and Mrs. Bow organize a party, exhibit family photos, offer building blocks and helpful suggestions, erotic puns, barbecued ribs, awkward noises, etc. Now we can see he is entirely conventional and solid. A hard worker, he would make a lovely anchorman. For this reason he might be the cause of disjunctive pleasures—being kept waiting at the gate, for example, or getting through the gate accidentally, or causing a scene at the gate. He is our newest enthusiasm. Two generations ago there was a new enthusiasm for buying on credit. We filled the town with large equipment for storage, refrigerators, interior decorations to establish coziness, batons, Variety Paks, disposable bowls, wood-paneled televisions, decorative pottery, and other highly processed, artificially structured, textured, and flavored versions of the original natural products. We bought motorized skewers so we wouldn't have to turn our hands. Today, there are minimal trails for hiking and horseback riding. Other natural landmarks are kept as protected landscapes, bounded by chain-link fences. We frequent them for concerts or picnics. On the way home there's a washing machine in the middle of the highway, and from the top of a nearby peak you can see the expanse below as a kind of horizon, a popular playground, glittering at dusk, and some of the residents can even afford their own special piece of the hillside. Haywood says, "Fill in the blank." I find him in different rooms; I find him with my own ears, eyes, taste, and smell. I find him and then I try to understand him better. I appear behind him in the mirrored closet doors, crossing my legs at the ankles. The following day, exposing habit to a different light, I come upon a dead squirrel in the gutter. This discovery provides two images in one moment of time: a wooden table and a shadow on the edge of a table. Who can explain it? The portrayal of flatness, at different moments, runs precisely from the interpenetration of past and present, the blending of colors on the eye. A sidewalk cannot be accurately drawn without leaving us with a vague picture of displacement, a palette of various objects in space at a given time: remnants of a past culture, assembled garbage, luster. One kid on the grass says, "Now what can I make happen?" Another kid says,

"Suck it." But Haywood has a sweetish taste I prefer to boiled beef; he can be tender and serve as a substitute for bread. He eats nuts and honey out of ceramic dishes. I diet for one week while he eats whole cornfields. At the store I buy berries, baked beans, fish, and pearl onions. I enter the room and say a simple good-morning. Like clockwork, we become excited by certain circumstances and styles. For example, I have an uncontrolled desire to organize. I spend dinner talking to myself and experiencing unexpected gleams of satisfaction. A century ago this would have been impossible; I wouldn't have even dreamed about it. I would have dreamed about shaking trees, or my chimney, or wasps, or trowels, or wiseacres, or a firkin of potatoes. Meanwhile, someone has taken to spray-painting the word *THIS* on street signs and mailboxes, no doubt one of the nameless kids. Their ability to choose is optimistic in its specificity. Stop *this*. Yield *this*. *This* over *that*. *Here* as opposed to *there*, or *nowhere*. A man stands back on his lawn with a dog. He tugs the leash and says, "She's trying to learn how to be friendly without being crazy." A sleek couple in spandex jog the sidewalk with aerodynamic baby strollers and Haywood seeks a return to Lasagna Tuesdays. We have arrived at a place based on the idea that the past never existed.

We set out intentions for public imagination, educational software, rumpus rooms, etc. Haywood makes dinner on an indoor grill. A bee flies up and down outside the window, bumping the glass, hovering above plates on the patio. Fruit is rotting on the trees, and the bee lives on after the death of the fruit. He is rejuvenated by past forms in my yard. He's a good sport. Just then a shy bird lands in the branches as I lean on my elbow. I'm so near the bird we're practically neighbors. All of a sudden there's another bird, a black one, and then two red ones, and then another that is both red and black. The two red birds face the black one, and I watch as they wrestle among the leaves. Then a fallen petal signals some sort of retreat. The red birds spring past me and out of the yard entirely. It was the only battle I've ever witnessed. That night Haywood seems to move toward a derisive nickname. He's perfectly right to do so. In the morning heat I look like pudding, or I sound like a mosquito squeaking under a mattress, or I fuck like a secretary with her hands full of paper. But I have sudden ideas like a fox, so many ideas, scenes, sudden beauty. So I sit on a cushion and write a letter to the seventeenth-century Dutch still-life painters, grouping them according to taxonomic phenomena: animals (pheasant, goose, dogs, cow, stag) and plants (melon, sweet cherries, leeks, gourds, pumpkin, blue grapes, lettuce, brambles, berries). The table has all its own categories: stale crusts of bread, wine stains, orange peels, stacks of plates, crumpled pink paper napkins, strawberry stems, dirty flatware, cat hair, walnut shells. I answer the phone twenty-seven times. "Who's there?" I say, but no one answers. It's like a sick and moody privacy, so I wear ruffles and read alone in the afternoon, fully absorbed by dangerous propaganda and fits of laughter. I flip through magazines that advise about weight loss, fashion, sexual dramatization, what is "hip" and what is "square." Unhappy people are analyzed with the latest vogues in impersonality. I eat a banana on my side by a tree. I smack my lips and shout at people who ride by in cars. This is incredibly exciting for me. Among certain groups of women, shouting at strangers has become a way to contrast oneself with particular social pressures. Lisle and I used to drive up and down Main Street on weekend nights in a kind of parade of increasing and decreasing speed, contraception, and overall total movement. Haywood played two outdoor sports. Today he is unlikely to participate in such customs. So I send him to the store to shop for milk, flour, and eggs. These are my own ideas about modern cake decorating: after baking, cool thoroughly, remove with caution; use the proper icing; the rose is the loveliest flower made with the tube. At different parties I see cakes that look like Barbie, or grand pianos, or golf courses, or Holiday Inns, or silver bells, or bowling alleys, or carousels, or hearts, spades, clubs, and diamonds, or guitars, or Bibles, or flags, or flowers, or duck hunters, or French poodles, or holiday baby booties, or hands in prayer, or horseshoes, or Girl Scouts, or clown heads, or patriotic fish, or race cars, or woven baskets, or country scenes, or psychedelic dancers, or the moon. There are different cakes for different occasions, some involving children, or sleeping children, or monster trucks, or battles for statehood. Meanwhile, there's a spatial plunge behind the dark oaks on the edge of town. The mayor wants to shut it down or build a fence around it. "It's like a dead word," he tells us. It's rumored all over town he cries in his sleep: "Wasted space!" Preparations are made. Grim men gather at city hall. This is only the first meeting. After a few days they manage to successfully redecorate the interior of the city offices. These are events of large civic significance and depend upon progress and reasons. That's the exciting thing. The whole town is interchangeable. Everyone listens to the same song at the same time, so we dance together under the stars (gold flecks in the ceiling). In bed that night I imagine a complex floral design with thin patches and some complete holes. I crank my arm faster and faster without brakes. Haywood says, "You are the victim of some mechanical metaphors." He has many possibilities available to him, things to talk *through*, and reasons to be suspicious. In the morning, I go outside and turn on the sprinklers. I stand in the driveway and imagine a morning just like this one, over one hundred years ago, when little Stella Duck ran past Mr. Edwin Stephens, so serious in his morning carriage, his glossy mustache and hat. She had a rag doll in one hand and a sack of flour at her feet. She was running into a house for protection from the rain. She had a round greasy face and a mop. Nearby were a rock and a log. There was a pine tree and a bluebird and a dog waking up. On the sidewalk a kid rolls past me with the smell of purple gum. I go inside and somewhere near the living room I remember a time when Lisle and I fell asleep with giant wads of bubble gum in our mouths only to find ourselves later in a pink sticky web. She wrapped herself in a blue-striped sheet in the bed. She looked "bedroomish." The question was whether the sun would dry the gum on our skin or if we'd have to sit tight and wait for someone to peel it off. In the end we had to stamp to keep warm. We went swimming in the lake and made tracks in the green grass. On the way home a car accident slowed traffic for nearly an hour. A dozen people stood around a dead body on the side of the road covered in a drab blanket except for its feet, and one shoe was missing. But I become distracted. Again, it's night. From somewhere upstairs Haywood says, "Beside the point," then "Wish." I wake to make angry demands on myself: feed orange peels to the garbage disposal for one hour. I visit the public library and pore over manuscripts and innumerable periodical charts and books. I learn to appreciate the small green lamps, and then I write aggressive letters of extraordinary vividness and humor. I write about the world and more, facts that impose themselves on our features, until it suddenly becomes clear this is like software running on a machine in my brain, so I return to my house (where really everyone has an equal chance of getting through the gate) and I'm useful for what must be five minutes (vacuuming, paying bills, making smoothies, etc.). Haywood says, "Your body is a machine." He can't distinguish between what's real and his own falsehoods. I don't even wait for him to finish. I walk to the train station. In the dark I find a new and interesting swagger; it's a kind of moral resistance and there might be other versions. So I think: now the whole town is asleep, everything. I observe it in third person. Dear Mrs. Pitt, If it wasn't such an important stage in this dramatic breakdown I'd tell you a secret, such as: this town is preoccupied with the dregs of society, with cosmic determinism, bondage, corsets, all sort of confinement, scrotums, bats. No one concerns himself with the truth because no one is worried about being absolutely important. We grow nostalgic. We sing songs and shout at strangers. This is incredibly sexy for us. Afterward we retreat to outdoor grills and the smell of commemoration fills the air. Dear Mrs. Sharp, I am one of the best letter writers in this town, if not *the* best. I was born here and never strayed. That's a lie. No one was born here. I am a rugged individualist and a sage. Thank you for attending my party. Dear Mrs. Saxton, There are many open spaces I hope to fill. I start with small holes in the yard—fill some in with yellow roses, jelly beans. I pour hot coffee into garden fountains. You once asked my opinion about Mrs. Ox. I can't tell you who hangs in her gallery of portraits. She opens and closes like the fish on a dock. I do nothing. I squeeze my eyes shut. Yours truly, etc. Haywood watches TV in the kitchen and I watch from the bath. He has a third manner, unlike his first two. In this other one, he cries at Hollywood endings and commercials on television for cameras or cotton. One movie features four kids and animals that speak with English accents and take their tea with milk. Another movie is about animals that talk, but these animals carry backpacks. Later, the strange newcomer sends me mixed signals in public spaces. He's good at his job and attracts people even doing nothing. I wear a textured cardigan with a matching or contrasting skirt. I wear a slash of red at the neck. Or an odd belt to define my waist. But I don't touch my eyes. I sip my wine through a straw. Then Haywood and I eat dinner in the backyard and listen to neighbors complain about heartburn. We watch neighbors in yards with children or dogs. In one yard, two kids float by on an inflatable raft, a brother and sister, the sister reclining while the brother rows with a fallen branch. The sister is slightly seductive—a pair of swimming goggles dangling from her right hand, her left hand resting casually on her left hip. The brother is thinking about water, and extra water, and more water, and island castaways, and island economies, and bittersweet victories. He says, "Let go." He was baptized in that very swimming pool. Haywood goes to bed early. I carry a pair of scissors from one room to the next. I spend most of the evening holding the scissors and looking at a fig tree in the neighbor's front yard. Dear Mr. Mayor, I suppose you expect me to begin with some shocking new discovery. I see your car parked on the street outside my house as I write this. Does that shock you, Mr. Mayor? In particular, Mr. Mayor, the extraordinary discourse that you insist on forcing before me, it disturbs me. My own vehicle is washed clean. Do you get me? The velvet curtains in the front room have been shampooed. There is nothing left to discover. It was an affecting and truly a good first try, but please desist in your attentions. I'm afraid I must be firm. Sincerely, etc. On the evening news they find a body in the reservoir, funneled through a series of irrigation ditches—from grove to field to lake (recreation area). Babies stand in the water in plastic diapers. I move around the house like an animal, one that doesn't frighten easily, and one that swings its limbs pretty aimlessly when it walks, or like an animal that seems to swing aimlessly but actually has a clear and definite ambition. I say, "Family romance," then "Three glasses," then "Bingo!" Haywood walks past me on his way to the bedroom. I say, "You're swell. The swellest." Afterward I cook dinner but the smell of it makes me sick. Haywood says, "I'm waiting on the second floor!" The rest of the night I appear to be quite at home. I stand before one window with a kind of affection. Then I dream that any civilized man can hire me to clean his copper pump. With seemingly aimless movements I pass flowerbeds, but with freshly painted fingernails I force open layers of green-blue petals until they emerge like sick, wordless tongues. A bird sounds like plastic whistles. Inside, the hero of my story throws plates and wet sponges. The next question is: How much happier do you want to be? Haywood marches. He says, "I have rights!" He's like a mathematical object or religious dogma. In indirect speech I say "this" seven times and "that" nine times. It's called *le discours indirect libre* in France; it's also an angle of vision. I hold forks and knives. Pretty sharp! The petals are twisted open to make signatory remarks. I watch them from the kitchen window. My sink is the object of my own contemplative gaze. Outside, there is a white cotton shirt in the middle of the street, twisted up with fallen leaves, which could be my shirt. It could be mine. It could have fallen out of my bag when I crossed the street. But suddenly it's trash. Suddenly it's disgusting, like a long hair on the edge of the bathroom sink. I walk right past it. I walk past a stray dog on the sidewalk, ignoring its damp snout and ponderosity. I bump up against walls and fences. This place is an ill-defined and monotonous kind of dreaming. The sound on the streets is plastered over by bay windows and back gardens. My own closets are deep and full. I filled them with hats and books and other sub-cultural forms, sixteen clocks, monogrammed blankets, skirts with furry rims, different things with different colors, plum-colored towels, ballet flats, fuzzy dice, posters of dolphins, skates, etc. Now I roar up. I say, "Frozen peas." I say, "Pulverized," then "Extinction!" then "I would hate that." Instead of learning from our mistakes, we continue to build in the exact same way. There's a school in the middle of an area where they want mountainous hotels. But no one's a crystal ball. To celebrate we want another parking lot, a bigger lot, with bigger spaces, and many good spaces close to the entrance. It takes paperwork and months and more paper. The mayor says, "Indefatigable!" We bulldoze small and inconvenient fields of strawberries or corn and replace them with the increasing complexity of everyday life: promised lands, the right of "choice," boundaries, color schemes, paper mills, etc. There are golf courses, chain restaurants, six brand-new gated communities, and, in the edge-towns to the north, there is a debate about public housing and how to shift responsibility for the poor. The book calls it "suburbanizing the conventional inner city," and argues that it is "excessively intentional." But this place is a flat surface. This place is distinct from other places and at the same time isn't. This place is really convenient. There are all sorts of differences that already exist. The book tells us we resemble virtual neighborhoods and according to the experts the virtual is "more compelling" than we are. I walk through streets and look in windows to witness cheerfully painted walls and vertical lamps, high technical quality and surround sound, mystery, beauty, fry baskets, fried chicken legs, joy sticks, shelves, ovens, beans. Over and over I encounter specific signs, such as Prepare to Merge. I stand in front of one public mural entitled *The Evolution of Dishes*. But a blue heron flies over my car and then just disappears. I carry on for weeks after this. I squeeze oranges into paper cups for vitamins. I cluster near the base of bedside lamps. It's like I can't rest confident in the political circumstance of one small space, this one, or right outside the window, or across the street, or over by the train station. As if I'm delicate. As if I'm deserted. As if I'm an endangered ocelot or a farmer on a stamp. As if I identify randomly with people on the street. As if I'm named Yvonne or Yvette. As if I have a bright pink refrigerator. As if I'm exhausted or superstitious or aggressively sexualized and armed with an assortment of lasers or guns. I don't feel a thing. In the morning, over coffee and eggs, I'm exhorted to be an individual. In the afternoon we wash our cars. At night I'm restricted to a relatively confined social circle. The cat climbs in and out of empty boxes in the hall. I sleep with the window open and imagine. Tonight a celebrity on television mentions his wife and kids. He tells the camera he spent last year riding a motorcycle around the world. His favorite color is purple and his card is American Express. Tonight I deny my ordinary life. I converse with the very words. I impress myself on men's hands as I make my way toward the restrooms at the back. I drop my dress on the floor. I chop produce. I pick weeds. I pop a plastic bag for no real reason. I take advantage of particular events, of particular sentiments, to render a particular series of events. I become detached from the routine of lawn, lawn, office building, lawn or "Bring me milk," "Bring me sugar." I say, "Milk me sugar" and "Sugar me milk." I move through the house and let my kimono slip open, a soaring kimono with silvery cranes and blossoms. I get the mail in my open kimono and meet the neighbors' stares with my own absence. There are bills and catalogues for garden furniture and candles. There is a letter written as a kind of crazy joke, it's a sort of contest, a contest. It's easily stirred. I leave the bowl on the counter and the bugs find it. "You're filthy," it says. It amounts to nothing. The season, as it progresses, becomes un-collective and un-plural. I acquire a certain understanding with the abandoned swimming pool in the park. It contains a distinctive temperature, a soft molecular surge. In bed I can feel it (strange nighttime rhythms). In the morning a pebble sinks (pebbles and crows). Meanwhile, the evening news is a whole nightmare of the future involving underground laboratories and weather. What is buried in our thoughts is self-evolving. Out there is a continuity of something; it is secretly allowed to cross borders and nations. The book in my hands says, "You wouldn't like to live on a coral reef but sometimes you would." I cool my face against the beveled edge of the glass table in the living room. I stand on the table and look out the window. I bruise my leg on the glass edge. So I carry my work into another room where there are decadent lamps and signs of Egyptology as a hobby. Apparently, we are vulgar popularizers of the superficial. Sometimes we don't even know it's happening. Other times I feel it rise up in my throat like a genteel wrath. Haywood's flapping smile is wholly innocent.

And what's left? What one might wonder is: Is this fast trip through my own little strip of time my own? Am I on it? One day someone will decode intricately wrapped gifts on the far limits of the tabletop: glass grapes, bunches of plastic marigolds, a blue plate, a white plate, a heaping pile of fallen petals. In the movie of my life I'll play myself, from a distinct past, or a gliding distance, in the garden, under a stone bench, or from the leaves like a watchtower. It's enjoyable—the rising and falling of large ideas we play off against our bodies. Like that thing there, can I put it in my up or down? There are breakfast plates, a fork, a knife, a chunk of bread, paper napkins, a banana sliced in half and standing on end. Later, on the same table, there's a chocolate bar wrapped in blue-and-silver foil, a pear. I stand in my house. I collaborate with the window and fill it optimistically with my figure or silhouette, which is somewhat rewarding. Other days I am ragged and gross. I move into the night and arrive at stones. Then I move southward through an idealized artificial system. I attempt to single-handedly reinvigorate the relationship between people and place. I shake myself on the sidewalk like a dog. I am prominent and astounding, but everyone else is asleep. I stand in the light from lamp-posts and point at revivals of traditional architecture, landscape scenarios, bifurcations of community, etc. All the houses have at least one door. The initial idea wasn't ours, but we've incorporated it totally. When I get home, Haywood is in bed. There is a pain in his chest and he does not choose to perform for me. I eat cake and stand in front of the window in the kitchen. There is something in the backyard, in the dark, so I go outside and squat in the grass, but whatever it is runs away from me. In the morning we go back to the kitchen to eat breakfast. First, one person gets up and goes into the bathroom. Then someone else showers in the bathroom after dinner. In this way, each moment corresponds to a different room. On the evening news they show clips from the nation's largest machine-gun show. There are vendors selling automatic weapons with mass-market appeal and teenage boys in camouflage spraying bullets at an old Cadillac. Families walk by the camera smiling and waving and eating chunks of meat or corn. There are baseball hats and ski-caps and ponytails that sway and look soft. Then the reporter interviews a man with a metal cashbox and a rifle over his shoulder. Later, Haywood and I sit in a swing and look out at all our grass. A bird sings at us from his perch in the tree, but the nests he builds will fall into the pool when it rains. There are all sorts of flowers in the hedges—

edible, highly scented and purple—and red clogs for gardening. If stitched together, the lawns on this street would be pointless and unrecognizable. Three houses down, one hostess serves champagne and eggs. She carries cupcakes on small trays and the wallpaper in her kitchen is a repetitious pattern of carrots and peas. I keep trying to lie down on all her furniture. Around midnight Haywood and I lock our door with a bolt. We have the right to choose which bodies will enter this special community and which bodies will be denied entrance. For example, there are carefully maintained areas devoted to leisure, areas that measure more than five feet across and that are bounded by special functions. But that's just it. Sometimes it seems this place is an assortment of ordinary, illiterate people who grew up eating crops. Sometimes we root ourselves in limitations that seem relatively straightforward. The main difference is that if you never leave you are always already here. Sometimes it's exhausting, or sometimes it's straightforward in a blank way, like fear. Meanwhile, Haywood is poised between one great idea and one general. I feel his frustration like the brainless grace of a goose capsizing. Then again, it's as if he admires how I sit in the dark in the midst of my failures. He wants me to. Instead I sit on the porch under an abstract specimen of sky, stretched out. I continue reading: "'Good God,' she cried, 'the violets down below!'" What he finally decides is that what we have is a kind of awkwardness worth saving. His systematic attempts to be a husband are my instructions for the next few hours. We move behind the couch where he presses his fingers against my neck. He puts his toes in my vagina. "Good God," I cry. I lean against the wall. My face is probably magnificent. My cunt in the moonlight. Afterward, we eat pasta with cream and only use one bowl. Haywood leaves his shoes on the kitchen floor. He showers downstairs. I stand in the living room in front of the open window. The sidewalk grows bigger and bigger. I see it reaching up through the window, growing bigger in the moonlight. "How do I look?" it asks. We could take a train together and disappear in the city outside. It's impossible; it lies outside the envelope of my own special case. So in a little while I lose my head on the sidewalk, in the lamplight. An owl plunges from the branches toward the asphalt and via a series of similar accidents I lose my head. The following week there is a documented sexual encounter on that very sidewalk. Two people embrace in full daytime view of a wide range of neighbors. These are people we know, but do not know. So I step away from the window and breeze past a lot of furniture. I breeze past a table in the corner covered with knickknacks. I return Haywood's shoes to their appropriate spot. I straighten one framed photograph on the wall and place a pitcher of water, several kiwis, and a dozen or so blue petals on the edge of a different table in a completely different room. Then I sit down and push the tablecloth away from me, about two feet away, and wipe the surface with a wet yellow sponge. For lunch I eat several olives, a quail, three loaves of bread, and a sausage, and then I read through old letters in full view of the city, or in the garage. My views move to another room, always different, sometimes, or individual, a pull of some history (tonight the presence of a storm). But the letters carry on, hoping to probe our smoothed-out-sense-of-self. They augment an unstatic perception. I watch the city through the gaps in trees. The city is an actualizing background for all kinds of arbitrary treatments. On the edge of my view is a communication, a light, a quick boom. I pretend to be increasingly deaf—in this way I put Haywood in a little book in the dark. I can't pass it. I can't possess it. I defeat myself in an afternoon, so I stalk monarchs across the lawn with a net. One kid says, "Happy birthday!" Another says, "Trick or treat." The social-historical importance of this place is tenuous, and thus, necessarily, has a clear and definite aim. I produce documentary objects: Historical Varieties (i.e., Verities), apple pies, sexual feelings. I make a diaper out of plastic wrap and ask Haywood to wear it, but he won't. He is one resident who supports social distinctions. He says, "What do you have to say for yourself?" We sip green cocktails and wait. Family meanings inflect these conversations. We listen to one member of the family who talks about airport safety. Then we go into hidden parts of the house or yard and cross-fertilize like birds and squirrels or like the work in any beanfield. Pesky neighbors show up on our lawn after dinner. This is evidence of the demise of my easy world, which *seems* like it's easy. For dinner I serve roots, pumpkins, radishes, and kale. I garnish it with red onions, parsley, and mint. We are culpable, hateful. We sit back and pick off spiders walking the circumference of our town during the autumn months. But sometimes we share a vision, we pick out a criticism, we plunge ourselves into compassions of indistinct sensation: change, transfer, dazzling. Dear Mrs. Moor, You are marvelously entertaining. For more than thirty years you have beguiled us. Mrs. Moor, you are scandalous and a monster. You are our classiest delinquent. The way you sit, Mrs. Moor, the way you eat noodles or curry, the way you serve a large piece of meat, and the way you always look so fresh. Mrs. Moor, you remind me of a girl I knew who woke up one night with a strange tingling in her mouth. She walked down the hall to the bathroom and opened her mouth and spit out a bee. What is your secret, Mrs. Moor? What is your favorite color? Warmly, etc. I am absorbed into a place where people make themselves up out of certain images or mediated public phenomena. I lose control of my speech and am forced to disentangle myself from organized group activities. With sunlight behind them, the leaves on the trees are awkward shapes. Someone in the town thinks of me while eating boiled potatoes, and then someone thinks of me while folding paper cranes. In this way the neighborhood is as entertaining as kittens or a cultural exhibition or the derivation of the word *engastration* (the stuffing of one bird inside another). Dear Mr. Surgeon General, I saw a puppy stuff his nose into the green grass. Everyone loved it. I stuffed my nose in the grass, Mr. Surgeon General, and it sank down, motionless, and lay for a second on something vaguely round right down there near the path. I wanted to tell you, my body is an inhospitable host for any living thing—even colds. When my neighbors turn spotted and yellow and loll around with thick waxen bodies, I feel great. Sincerely, etc. Really I'm shocked to discover I don't even want to accomplish my goals. I associate myself with the American frontier and sort of want to enclose myself in some small nomadic unit. I migrate over sidewalks and lawns. Then I supply sexually constipated and hypocritical citizens with all kinds of bonuses and obligatory rituals. For example, there's the fact that the most important part of me will never even be seen. I can say about it: "This is my own primary interest," or "I'd rather be a goose in Canada." This is what it means to be a national grown-up. It's a kind of supportive and spontaneous process involving naive, imitative, and prudish culture. Its critics and creators seem to just go on living. At night, from my position on the front porch, I see it as a vast complex of apocalyptic foreboding. I twirl my hair and chew on the tips. Even in the dark, my arms and legs and teeth are present; I talk with my hands and am portrayed as communicative or right or passive or contemporary or undefended or conscious or uncritical or disturbing or disinterested or dangerous or self-respecting or old-fashioned or a mixture of things, like network programming, depending on the channel and the time of day. It's not surprising the streets follow a circular craving. In the dentist's chair

I think of walking the sidewalks at sundown. It's an unseasonably warm day and my impulse is to take off my clothes and swim in all the pools. I can't open bottles for whole days, or then I can't get them closed. Weird smells come and go. I'm unable to distill sections of my life I'd rather leave out. But inside the bottles? I don't know which one to choose or how to tie it down. Then I bump into the strange newcomer, who says he admires my hunger. We say hello and goodbye in several kitchens. We stand in front of one table on which a green glass bowl, a silver bowl, an apple core, one cranberry, a brown stain, and a brandy snifter etched with gold are clustered in the corner. Around this time I speak frankly with many gentlemen of favor. It's an apparently simple feat. Of course, every man I know knows much less than I know, which is why they want to know me, but it means they'll have difficulty performing without feeling foolish, for hours even. One man in particular is mute before me. He rejects everything that is "frivolous" and pretends to be a pilgrim. He sits on our couch with a glass in his hand and speaks of infrastructural development and assessment, other passions, his wife crawling over him. He gets up and mentions my charms: a gold and silver sun-and-moon combo. He pulls at his penis through his pocket. He does not have to be so unappealing. He should think up a way to prove himself worthy of an expression on my features, on any one of them. So I excuse myself to feed my guests at the touch of a button. I feed them bananas and walnuts, and then I feed them turkey, stuffing, biscuits, horseradish, crackers, pork, French toast, cake, mushrooms, spaghetti, sweet potatoes, fish, and green-bean casserole. Originally, I thought: Haywood and I are fond of each other in the way a child likes sudden changes. Still, the elements of a system have significant patterns. We move from room to room, sometimes for a whole day, without conversation. We arrange objects in patterns on tables and come along to disrupt patterns of papers, utensils, cupcakes, plates. Or we circle the furniture in seemingly dissimilar patterns the immediate social functions of which are unclear. I hold sharp objects in the middle of the kitchen—knives or toothpicks—just to be sure he knows the distinct causal order of our discrete little world. Then his appearance in another room is like the appearance of an appropriated subject. In this way Haywood might as well be sitting at a table in someone else's still life, with fish bones and a box of apple juice or an empty shaker of salt. I go for a walk. When I return there is a letter. The letter is an affair of deception and betrayal. I put it back in the mailbox, but they won't take it. I decide to learn two foreign languages. A third seems unnecessary. I say to a dog on the sidewalk, "Bandito," and "Sure, sure." Then I see the mayor and he means business. His shoes are ridiculously gleaming; however, his admiration for my rigorous epistolary style makes me respect him. At an oblique glance he follows me across the street and into a phone booth. He is brilliant at acting like he needs to borrow something. I can paraphrase what he said. He said, "Should I take my hat off?" In other words, "Is this place inside or out?" I ask him what he wants to say and he whispers, "Nothing." Meanwhile, in a yard across the street a life-size inflatable polar bear wears a purple hat and bobs on the grass. Cars arrive in clumps. Pigeons peck at dirt. Night comes and Haywood returns from the city. He says, "Just that, just so." On the countertop is a plastic container of beets, half a red onion, a crumpled paper towel, a slice of lime. The phone rings its musical ring and Haywood answers, speaks in muted tones. I pick roses in the backyard and offer them to a crystal vase in the front room on a mahogany table beside a globe lamp and a picture of Haywood on vacation. The roses are sweet-scented and spiked. I stare at them between my fingers from farther down the hall. I grew up in a house crammed with preserved fruit and we joked about the wallpaper. But my new hat, it's a kind of originality, an accident. I wear it. I wait on the sidewalk. "Come inside," I say. This is what happens after days of gigantic smiling. A person ought to know better. I say, "What do you mean 'yuck'?" Haywood has an appointment in the city. I count the plates. On the table in the hall are two candlesticks, a cake stand, and several heirloom tomatoes. There are dirty dishes in the kitchen sink and a rice cooker on the floor. So I decide to count the number of steps from our front door to the first duck standing upright on the half-frozen pond in the park. But I see the strange newcomer and he does not step out of my way. Today's the day it's fated this theater will open our eyes to insensible things (sprays of white flowers near the base of nearby trees). Together we leave the gravel path, showing signs of nomadic tendencies inherited from the earliest settlers. We move west through the park and conquer it in geometrical shapes, a grid of squares and rectangles, find a parcel of land to call our own and stick a flag in the dirt. We squat on the ground to complete the exercise. Everything around me swells to mythical size. So the rocks are mountain ranges and the bugs are bald eagles. I imagine my own face is reflected in the skies and trees. I imagine the world is wholly transformed. I imagine I emit a fine fragrance, like lemon trees or kittens, and that all nature is my companion, and I am more elastic and immortal than ever. Then the sky grows starry and I momentarily bless myself and dig my fingers into a soft cradle of dirt and moss. Tragically, when I leave the park alone, the grass is easily destroyed by the regular expanse of the sole of my black leather shoe and all the geese point me in one direction, constantly. In a kind of embracing-time they point me *that way*. So I brush myself off. I head south. On Main Street I step over newspapers scuttling the street. "Today in History" a school was erected. "Today in History" a colony of muskrats was discovered in a meadow. "Today in History" a house was demolished; a sergeant was killed in war. "Today in History" the water on Center Street was ten feet deep. Suddenly, there is a large stuffed rabbit high in the branches of an oak tree. The rabbit is bright pink, tremendously pink against the backdrop of the bright blue sky. It's too awkward to realize what's wrong. There's something in the hedges. There's someone touching himself on the grass. I move down the sidewalk and pass garage doors and snapping flags. Then I eat brown butter sauces, fish, spinach, apples, lamb, lemons, tomatoes, mushrooms, fingerling potatoes, carrots, garlic, and thyme. I eat confectioner's sugar and salt. I eat pomegranates, grapefruit, persimmons, a pinch of cayenne pepper, sesame seeds, popsicles, marshmallows, and chips. I stay on top of trends. I try new window treatments. I keep my houseplants thriving. I sort my jewelry by size and color. One kid says, "I don't like it." Another kid says, "Shit." Still, the women, they weep all the time. They do it on television or in the middle of the street. I'd shake them, but it's not as if we're deserted here. We all agreed to this. One husband even composed a song for the occasion. Dear Mrs. White, To begin, there are two kinds of rose gardens—there are rose gardens belonging to those for whom roses mean money, and there are rose gardens belonging to those for whom roses mean fun. Depending on the season and the climate, cut roses can be placed in the middle of the table or on the edge, beneath an open window or beside a bowl of nuts. Roses might be pinned to dresses or slipped singly through buttonholes. This was a ready symbol for courtship years ago, as was crinoline, clean cars, socks, pointy breasts, and all the things you see in movies. It was loads of fun, or so I imagine. Sincerely, etc. Soon Haywood and I throw a party. I strap myself into the kitchen and press "Go." I time Haywood's embraces. The cat sleeps all the afternoon with forbidding coolness, like a surveillance camera. I sit on the carpet in front of the fireplace and listen to planes overhead. But don't forget, there's a conversation underway. Haywood is forthright. He's into concepts that evoke images, of rocket-pearls, or something like that, of achievements anyway, like equipment, clamps. Outside there are markers, observable, fixed in space—pretty little lights that illuminate conspicuous circles of gravel and grass. They've occupied my attention throughout most of this. Meanwhile, that tree outside the window can be sad if I think it so. If not, I might think everything is fine, so the tree is, the roof with the squirrels on it is, everything is fine even if a fire engine comes down the street as fast as possible, that tree is green and I am full of compassion. What a nice tree. Everyone says so. I can't even decide if I'm one of them. Whatever else it means it means I'm more or less consistent. I buy the things they sell and sort of want to forget about it. I walk a track through the neighborhoods: Oak Manor, Stonebridge, Indian Creek Estates. I let the sidewalk carry me and observe garden furniture, model homes, archipelagos of homes, 91 percent homeownership, fireproofing, ornamental street lighting, fallen leaves, this "miracle town," etc. Meanwhile, I receive postcards from the strange newcomer with a deep sense of formulation and affix them to my closet walls. As they accumulate I will have to read a structure of sentences with an emphasis on alignment and metaphors that don't bear much examination (a sweet golden prize). On one, a question: "Do we communicate subsensically to *practice* communicating so that we can understand each other when we need to?" When the time comes? Then I have a dream in which I have to put my shoulders *on*, like a scarf, so that the cats will run into *me*. On the table is half a grapefruit, a small pile of coffee grounds, an almost empty glass of milk, a fork, a spoon, a plate, a blackening banana peel. The book in my hands says, "Question your teaspoons." A kung fu master on TV says he can screw himself into the earth and then unscrew. Maybe it comes in handy where he's from. In this place, the police station is next to the liquor store, which is illuminated with a buzzing neon F. People go past it. People walk quickly off. People pull down on each other. They must be the sociologists of the era, sorting through crusts, interior decor, insurance claims, etc. The whole town has the strongest need to wrestle in the bushes. We meet out there after sundown. One kid pees in his bed. I power through lifestyle manuals and other suggested fantasies of self-recreation. I take cues from my television for ways to have a blank stare. Then, and quickly, there's stillness in the air. Haywood asks me to re-create all the meals he ate as a kid. On the corner of the table is a blue-and-white plate with three green pears and beside it are two apples in shadow. I drink a can of cola and leave the tab on the edge of the countertop beside jellied fruit candies made with sugar substitute. I walk the street. I walk it and as I walk it I am totally adult and reasonable. I pass a fallen branch. I pass one family with ten children. I look back and see the same family in a friendly argument on the sidewalk. I can't get inside their conversation. I migrate from place to place. I go too far in one direction and then I turn around. In the morning I am acrimonious for no particular reason. I brush my hair and situate myself before a landscape of specific social and cultural significance. In the mirror I see a shoulder draped by a shawl, and in the next room I see a window onto a garden, and in the garden below I notice lots of things without even looking. Mostly, my eyes serve to classify and legitimate things. For example: on the dining room table is a roll of wallpaper waiting to be applied, a glass of water, a spoon, a cracked pomegranate, a crumpled paper napkin, and a whole host of crumbs (yellow and dried). It should be clear that the glass of water threatens to fall off the edge of the table at any moment. But Haywood stands very still, which indicates change is unlikely. He holds staplers and lives here about three hours each day. There are vital political concerns to the evolution of this place and its inhabitants—obvious social functions are the least of it; there are other factors, moments of rediscovery, individual work. Consider my relation to the original inhabitants and all the local names. Millions of years have passed since turtles first crawled up on empty stretches of beach, like cars. When Haywood returns from a long day working toward similar evolutionary significance, I offer him a tangerine. We justify our mutual hatred by the confinement of this place, its houses and corners. It becomes segments of seeing and sensing (seething). I move under bridges and out to the edge. I explore what has already begun to recede. The world beneath my feet is a multiplicity of partial worlds. If I were to try to record an immediate impression of every lasting influence on my life I might find them in the gaps between *lying* and *sentiment*. Even the most tedious descriptions of this town might be of value. Even if I were its worst representative. I would have to be the hero, of course; I would have to draw maps of places and manners, but from the standpoint of the maintenance of necessary life. For example, the way the bathroom gets steamy, or how children humiliate one another. It can be seen in my letters to Lisle. I bind them with attractive blue ribbons. It might be that these letters are more satisfying to me than ordinary personal relationships. I now have three words in my mind, though often a vast variety of others. On the dining room table is a sea-green tablecloth and also a white tablecloth, as well as one wine goblet with pinkish liquid and a differently shaped goblet with a touch of green in the glass. Also, there are half-eaten squares of Turkish delight, cherry stems, a trail of granulated sugar, three forks, a spoon. Dear Miss America, A child expresses delight. Though he lacks a sturdy skeleton, he seems authentic. This boy plays drums on empty canisters. He has a simple and oblique perspective. Away from this urban center he would be more ancient than much in my everyday world. He goes along, thinking, almost automatically. He is not coordinated, his body is suitable, but delicate, his left arm circles slowly above his head before coming down again on the empty drum. Meanwhile, my husband requires an electrical device, an energy-saving system, a versatile clock. I buy pineapples and the water line on my shoe is evident from an afternoon walking along the shore. Seabirds return to the surface clutching things. Warmly, etc. Dear Mrs. Marcus, I am sorry to hear you won't be able to come again, but don't mistake this for a different type of apology. Let us consider another threshold: a creature with claws. Of course I don't mean it. I appreciate the fruit you brought from your tree. Please accept these flowers as representing the nature of my sensibility regarding your tragic, or should I say ironic, hesitation. Yours, etc. Seen from above, there is a peculiar pattern to our expansion: neighborhoods snake around supermarkets, hospitals, airports, malls. It's wanting to not be left behind. Houses shimmer together with the weather. There's a kind of earthy gravity to the weather. I uncover this fact by accidental research. I figure I might have an internal architecture, with buttresses, abundance, possibility, or an intestinal space in which nothing works the way it should, like buildings built on botanical models, or buildings based on your own DNA, or whole rooms built to laugh in, or sticky gardens with the usual material but brighter, or more dull. I could offer ripe fruit to the nameless kids, or mini-quiches, or scarves, or I could take them by the hand. On the kitchen counter are faded lily stems, white-faded, translucent in water, and tipped over, with yellow-orange spores streaking the cabinet to the floor. Nothing I do can deceive; the curtain is rendered convincingly in relation to the stereo with its red blinking lights, the heavy desk, the rug and couch. It's all in the eye, the beauty of the suburbs, its sharp whitish light, the lack of logical relationships; it's been written about in local circles or schools. It's a corner of nature demonstrated by bulldozers, machines, tractors, etc. It's been recorded by accident, on film or video to preserve the years, the human marks, signs of light and air, an intuitive kind of creativity. Meanwhile, Haywood is undergoing subtle changes. He mumbles quietly in unknown parts of rooms. I watch from shrubs. Though I try to maintain a certain reserve it's impossible to be cool searching for someone in a darkened movie theater or walking through a web. Dear Mr. President, Hello. The month is not celebratory. The changes are suspicious. I am tempted to offer a general abstraction as my excuse: one part preoccupation and three parts ongoing debate. You know what I mean, Mr. President. I am particularly involved in learning to do things for the first time. What would you recommend? In the news today they reported that women with heart-shaped faces look especially good with a bob. Also, I learned that it's better to do your shopping when you have a clear idea of what you want. Sincerely, etc. I stand in front of the washing machine and eat a blood orange off a small white plate. I leave the plate and the peel on the edge of the counter and drink water from a tumbler and wipe my hands on my pants. Then I take the warm laundry out of the dryer and carry it into the living room. This is a program inaugurated over a century ago and handed down, which may help to account for its differences from other work that it resembles. These are private routines not visible in census data. I locate my body by grounding it against the bodies of others. I am interested in knowing about all the possible thresholds. Walking through the mall there is a scene in which a woman in red leans forward to hand an item of purchase to a man in a brown coat who stands behind a table covered in folded sweaters of various colors and wicker baskets filled with rolled silk ties under which a small child sticks his hand into a plastic bag until his arm disappears. It might signify a larger trend in American culture: lawn-mower racing is becoming a regular sport—the importance of putting the pedal to the metal, deafening, this special race, geared-up, drawing millions, the magnitude of lawn care, its own kind of prim-and-proper. One kid says, "Haven't I built a good thing?" Another kid says, "Take that off." On the kitchen table there's a side of beef, yogurt, canned peaches, rice, pancakes, butter, a loaf of bread, a coffeemaker, a salt-shaker, S.O.S, canned corn, and several shiny peppers; the refrigerator door is open and inside is a frosted chocolate cake; above the refrigerator is a plastic clock in the shape of an owl; behind the table is an open window covered by gauzy curtains through which can be seen several mown lawns, deciduous trees, potted plants, and a sky-scraper in the far, far distance. So I drizzle beans with vinegar and work with side dishes and main dishes, such as chicken with thinly sliced carrots and parsley. This is a good dish to bring as a guest, if you follow my tips and advice. Then Mrs. Davis throws a Cookie Swap. There are prizes for the most unique packaging as well as the most original recipe, which goes to a chewy chocolate cherry cookie from the woman around the corner. I bring pecan date bars in a small basket with a linen napkin, which goes more or less underappreci-ated in the community of packaging panache and citrus tea punch and cookies more and more enticing: orange walnut tassies, rasp-berry windowpanes, pistachio lemon cutouts, chocolate meringue puffs. I exchange recipes with partygoers and return home in the snow. The city lights are throbbing through the empty treetops, like stars in the orbit of some other sky. I stare at the ceiling as I describe it to Haywood, who has the extraordinary capacity to be quiet. What so often separates us is ten dollars' worth of real Tupperware, an exhibited foyer, a brand-new Ford convertible, women dressed up as Cowboys and Indians, women in padded bras, women in gowns. Women put their hands to their throats, delicately, like aged tortoises. It's a whole thing of public opinion, sparkling bracelets, inequalities in height, and baggy necks, like toads on tiptoe. There's no real incentive to be sincere. So in an attempt to relax I think about white china on the breakfast table, chicken bones, a few dried petals from a flowering bush outside, a wet pink sponge, and the glare on the table from an east-facing window. Haywood holds a block of tofu. He says, "You are poorly dressed and very small." He says, "Remember your pockets. Remember your bag." What will become of us? There is a ruthless realism to the way we breathe, the way we sit at a table, the way we fuck, or eat breakfast, or sleep next to each other or next to thousands of strangers. This place has forgotten people living in other towns. We hardly recognize ourselves. "The rest," I say, "where is it?" I roll it inside my mouth. Each person I meet suggests a different answer to my questions. So, finally, I buy a white ceiling-fan to match the paint. It has gold knobs and chains, but what do I care? As one townsperson said, "It's a good example." The following day, I read a book by candlelight in the bathtub about attractive sexagenarians, and then on the couch I read a book about prairies and justice. Once, someone warmed the houses in this place with old trees, and they skated behind the stumps of old trees on the ice. But not these houses. People paid money for piles of wood or sticks; they played with stumps of trees after they cut them down; they jumped over the stumps for a game, or they threw axes at stumps and shouted "Hickory!" The park on the edge of town still has a grove of old trees in the midst of which it is difficult to distinguish persons or voices. Meanwhile, I think I scratched Haywood with my toenails in bed. Afterward I said, "What's so funny?" I said, "People who can afford to have it should have it if they want it." We work hard for what we love. In the morning I move sideways through the front yard; later, I move sideways up and down the stairs. I stand back and watch the door swing open. It looks just like an ordinary kitchen. A woman on television says she is more intense and less manageable since she started to be inscrutably inhumane. Another woman on television has a lot of trouble peeing. One woman on television screws lightbulbs into a lamp and she seems to really enjoy it. Another is just disoriented. One woman on television washes her face. One woman turns a faucet on and off. Another woman sues someone for sabotaging her in some way, for doing something unforgivable with a husband and a wig. Another woman sings about a bank. One woman is bloated. Another is doubled over in pain. A woman on television intensifies her brown hair with conditioning caramel tones. I sleep on the couch and dream I'm riding a bicycle away from the city quickly down a four-lane road in the dark when suddenly a pod of whales crests in the middle of the road and then plunges back down, which causes a huge asphalt-water wave that nearly knocks me off my bicycle, but doesn't. Nearby, Haywood feels the tragedy of a winter night like the dullest interval in the world. He makes creaking noises in some other part of the house. I resist the antirhetorical impulse to hurl paranoid, prefabricated abuse his way. The urge to criticize him is like a bad joke, and unambiguous. I break a plate and pull the fragments together. I am determined to speak to Haywood in a persuasive and controlled echo, like a radio announcer from the past. There are very few distractions other than these small sounds. We walk around them like invaders.

It's windy and the wind is so constant it's like being underwater. These are short afternoons and the best way to use them is to sit down with your thoughts. Then up comes a voice of wailing. I remember a story Lisle and I read about a prince and a bear, and another about an Egyptian man hatching eggs for his wife. I remember a lazy afternoon with Lisle. I remember afternoon turning into evening. I think the last thing I'd like to do is love nine thousand people. I walk in fog, then rain, then snow. The sidewalk takes me past driveways, water, weather, rivers. The sidewalk is an extreme form of dwelling in the river. I pick my way over sleeping cats and rocks and sticks. I hear bluebirds and squirrels and I strip to the waist and stand in at least six inches of pretty warm water. It laps at my calves and ankles. My skirt is saturated like a day after a warm rain. It was a day in July, on the 1st, or another day in July, or an evening in June on the 22nd, or about the 7th of July. Lisle wanted to forget about it. In any event, this place has grown over with a spongy kind of moss. I set my feet down in it. There are large fires and missing people and other things have broken up or floated off or just completely disappeared. The table is beautiful but it can be hard to recognize. It holds an amaryllis in a pot and a white saucer and a chocolate bar and two raspberries and a glass of wine. I part ways with it. With all the houses. With all the agreeable suburban parkways, I part. The following day we address ourselves with smiles and hidden purpose. It's like someone standing in the hallway or the tiny guest bathroom, just out of sight, holding a script, prompting lines or movements across the stage in a whisper. It's a creative form of alienation and one I look forward to as a personal kind of masterpiece. We see similar tendencies at the Culvers' holiday party. This sort of gathering gives the audience a closer view. The setting includes tinkling bells and candlelight. Everyone eats with a great deal of hand gestures while holding small arrangements of crackers or pie. Or else I'm making it up. Like the example of the donkey and the detective: I begin to find what I tell myself I will. I move along the street and my shadow is a line on the asphalt under the shaded light of lampposts. The following morning, a local man is sentenced to life in prison. Someone will probably write a movie about his crimes, unmotivated, the holy sinner, who brings us an awareness of ourselves. Meanwhile, on the street outside, two men shout congratulatory remarks in regard to the outcome of some game. Dear Mrs. McLuhan, The end of a tube of toothpaste can cause guilty feelings and a sense of alienation from progress. There are support networks for these sorts of things—feminine, domesticating—these parades of objects up and down, such as control-top pantyhose, handbags, lemon-scented versus unscented detergent. It's a question of family values. It's tempting to oversimplify such things, to associate them with syndromes or ailments. The opposing view stresses convenience and individuality. You make the call, Mrs. McLuhan. You consider the conceptualization of apples, acid peels, cereal boxes, and the virtues of commercial packaging that works like still-life painting on the fronts and tops of boxes. Warmly, etc. Dear Mrs. Noon, This is a neighborhood I know very well. When I arrive at a door, I ring the bell. I start conversations based on motivations, things that attract me, such as situations for discovery or frogs or fuel for fire. Also, I assimilate blank stares and could almost be said to be *happening*. You know it already, Mrs. Noon. In this sense I could almost be said to *have happened*. It's difficult to calculate the amount of time spent expressing ourselves strongly enough to be overheard. One hardly sees oneself. For example, one never sees one's own eyes. Do you see what I mean? I think you do, Mrs. Noon. Mrs. Noon, you are a person who invites compliments. You have a bird's house painted blue in your maple. You have a bowl of cherries on your kitchen table. You are like a familiar restaurant, and patient. However, I can't stop thinking about your worn-out leather shoes. I can easily provide the name of a reliable cobbler. Yours, etc. Dear Mrs. Pixley, I recall a remarkable walk we took one afternoon. It was a rainy afternoon in March or April. Or was it the summer? Was it July or August? All the same, Mrs. Pixley, it was a warm rain, and the walk resulted in a series of astonishing revelations. Don't you recall? Don't you remember the boy with balloons and the bizarre things that appeared: the plate of peaches, the lemon-yellow book on the edge of the sidewalk, the cucumber balancing on two turnips, the beautiful crystal vase with flowers and no water? Don't you remember these items? Don't you remember walking with me in the rain? It was a walk that led us north–west–north through familiar scenery. When I got home I waited for a few minutes in front of my own door. Always, etc. Dear Mr. Mayor, You were right. You can't stop it. You can't even act as if it were simply a gateway. The only practicable solution is to go on with the movement, day after day, just as we have seen. Mr. Mayor, I've been meaning to tell you that you came too late. I ordered various small salads and sat there perverted by an illusion of clarity or bliss. That is, a stupid realism eventually descended upon me, a kind of parody of the usual lunchtime entertainment only much, much funnier. You are a stooge, Mr. Mayor. I'm sorry, but it's better to end it this way than to come up with some new theory about the wise and kindly father figure. I wish you the best of luck with the wall you are building around your house. Sincerely, etc. Tonight on television people applaud furniture. They can't stop applauding it. They clap their hands together and then they open their mouths and shout. They say, "Woo!" and "Yeah!" and "Ah!" They applaud a lampshade and pillows ranging from $8.50 to $19.95. People don't know where to begin. The book says, "You can have it all," which might be what's so confusing. There's danger of a kind of disintegration. I shape and manipulate it. I set it on a cutting board. I pick it up and turn it over and then I desert it. After a while, it loses its special freshness. Then my life unfolds in reverse for a time. There is no other authority. I ask myself questions. I measure my memories and gestures and meditate on decay. One day rolls back on the next, and that one is covered in a rich color that has drained into it overnight. It has its origins in some event, hours prior, a breakfast or banquet, a scene at a table or on a sidewalk, or some sort of routine handling of sugar, dough, crops. Twenty years after the fact, I remember every piece of china I've ever broken. The one with grayish lines on the bottom, and the one shaped like a seashell, and the one that was holding the fruit, and the one with the spirals of red and pink, and how I sat there staring at it on the ground. In this way I almost interview myself and experience my whole life story and the story of people adjacent to me, or before me, and how people actually cope with opening up the land, and cats or clothes, and X-rays, and how they said that Tupperware was "the nicest thing that could happen to your kitchen." On the television a man says the bathroom should be filled with things that are tactile, beautiful, and large. This is no doubt due to his appreciation of some new luxury item. I bathe in a soft light because of the seemingly innocuous nature of this arrangement. I feel modern and full of life. I dust myself with candied fruits and stand on the edge of the tub from six to eight, or sometimes even for nine hours. It is a remarkably photographic setting. On the bathroom countertop are several aspirin cut in half, a glass of water, pink and blue cotton puffs, a golden bottle of perfume, and small soaps shaped like snails. Tonight, Haywood's breath is a mixture of beans and ice cream. The cat is thinking about dogs. I buy him tiny mice stuffed with catnip, but he doesn't care. He's like a familiar uniform when he comes into the room. All sorts of events happen at the same time but don't have to. I sit in the sun and absorb the weak rays and view the earth. On the kitchen counter are three glasses, two spoons, half a pecan pie, a box of detergent, a folded blue dishtowel. Haywood does different things for a variety of reasons. Meanwhile, I watch a film involving a murder mystery and someone lying about a murder. There are ghosts who actually hurt people, and ghosts who just chronicle what they know: foxes, gangrene, the peeping of frogs, the building of houses and the tearing down of houses, Christmas parades, confinement, mother-o'-pearl tints, games, sounds, ponds, trapdoors. Some ghosts carry faded marriage photos and a timeless sense of years, the ravages of years, of weaknesses, grassy knolls, high school yearbooks, marching bands, and other important points in history. Later, I watch a movie about a group of women in ancient China. It inspires me to reimagine my life, as if I'm standing in a pagoda in the woods, and there are shrines, and it's misty and green in the summer *and* the winter. On the dining room table is a dish of melted ice cream, a bag of candy, and two spoons. On the kitchen table: a butcher knife, a plastic cup, a kiwi. On the kitchen counter: a metal strainer, a green glass bowl with two peaches inside, a plastic cutting board, several jars, plastic bags, paper towels, a knife, a spoon, a bottle cap, a piece of cheese, and an apple. Out on the street four kids in bright colors run with a small brown dog on a leash. The children are of various ages and sizes. One kid says, "Stop, stop, stop, stop." At another house I pass a red dog in a black sweater, and then I find a cracked side-view mirror in the grass. I stand above it and look down at myself and my head against the sky, and then I stand on one foot on the edge of the sidewalk. I stand on my right foot, balancing, while I look down at myself looking back up. Then I open my hips to the north. I turn my torso north as well and place my right hand in the grass about six inches in front of my right foot. Also, I raise my left arm above my head. It takes a long time, maybe eighty-five years, and is the opposite of a snapshot.

AFTERWORD

I began the day reading the last words of a book so bright and lived in I didn't want to put it down when it was finished. There were too many sentences I wanted to keep for myself, too many threads extending from the book that wouldn't let me fill a jar with water or walk upstairs to shower without smiling, without tilting my head, without doing something utterly opposite: putting on a dress, drinking Kool-Aid. It was something Danielle Dutton could do that not many others had done (maybe Gertrude Stein had done it or Virginia Woolf): it was to write a world that was closed, that was full of everything you knew but also closed to your knowing yet electrified your knowing from across a field. You reached out of your body to read and everything you read seemed only to pertain to what was written. It was a closed system. The system was closed because the person inside the story only wrote what she saw and she mostly looked out of windows or mostly walked along sidewalks and often cooked meals and named meals and read books and wrote letters to neighbors. She was a wife at home. But the system also was closed because all other fields of description had been removed from language and what remained were lists of words that pointed to the home, to foods or clothing, to activity happening in the neighborhood—children playing, familiar people walking by with dogs, without dogs—and this language was what she had to make sense out of what she was seeing, which on one level was only suburbia and domesticity but on many other levels were ways in which various sites and actions were connected or the ways in which doing something opened up a tunnel in the mind, such that when our protagonist (we *are* in a fiction) narrates, "I walk through the doorway wearing my aggressively orange hat. I do it over and over. I do it as a kind of series and then I do it in reverse. I do it as an indicator of a particular lifestyle, to redefine myself and exclude others. First I do it in a red pantsuit and then I do it in the nude. I do it and I say, 'I doubt it'"—reading this I get caught up in the doing: she does, she does in reverse, she does with a point, she does differently, then does differently again, does one last time, then doubts it, the "it" being something spiraling off, concluding but making holes, too. And I realized I was reading inside a system that allowed me to do my favorite thing, which was to stop and stutter, which was to wrap the self around itself so many times that language creaked when it sought to put the self in motion: we do to move, we do to bridge, we do to leave a trace I had to think as I read that passage because now we were looking at the syntax of the body acting out narrative. But I also had to think if we looked at doing as a subject rather than an object pointing at a consequence, an arrival, an artifact then we might think how intricate it is to do, how fictional, how absurd, how infinite, how disastrous. A line lit up as I was reading and as I was making a distinction between what it's like to be a self indoors and a self out of doors, what you carried with you, what you did with your eyes as you walked, with your arms, what kind of pattern you made with your walking, and not only the eventual map that would evince itself (the streets, the turns) but also where you went in your thinking; and you could see as you read that there was a line burning a trail through the book and this line formed a boundary; yet rather than cut through the middle of the thing you were thinking—like, what's the difference between outside and inside—it weaved through the territory. The novel seemed to erase the time it took to get from one place to another. The period that closed the sentence was some kind of underground, and there was a line burning that became a place in itself. You began to feel that Dutton presented you with a surface—"There are all sorts of flowers in the hedges"—before she put a crack in it—"If stitched together, the lawns on this street would be pointless and unrecognizable"—then burned a line through—"I keep trying to lie down on all her furniture"—and these were moments that succeeded one another; they were a sequence of doing and observing, where on one hand you had this quirky story about the diversity of neighboring lawns being easily undermined by the aesthetic repetition of design then penetrated by unconventional behavior—on one hand you had that but on the other hand (though wasn't it the same hand, these were neighboring sentences) you had something straight go very crooked, and again this landed in the self: where you find the body in the day and in the mind. Which was the proper way to hold the book, you wondered as you read, and which were the things that were real to the narrator and which were real to the reader. Although, no matter how I held the book or in which order I read its pages, the surface of the narrative remained the most tactile of all other possible architectures, of any possible rising falling actions, of any horizons: I was moving through a world where every nominal thing, every act, every observation, every shift in time, every body passing the window, and every body occupying a room in the houses of this neighborhood was also an aggregation of marks on a surface, and one thing was a consequence of some other thing having happened or having been said to have happened; they flattened without hierarchy. And yet these same marks were bringing something to life that had nothing to do with the story you were reading but which used the story as its platform, as its place, and place was showing up everywhere and all of a sudden place was in you. The language did what it did to make a story and then it did this other thing that sort of glued the book to your hands: I was at least doubled as I was reading and could see objects in the novel doubling—though it wasn't so much that objects were doubling than that they were seeping, crossing through the terrain of every other object or back through themselves, vibrating plainly, and in this you could see how the sidewalk became "an extreme form of dwelling in the river," you could see how a cat's sensation of its "tiny feet" could bend "a sort of emptiness around." It was a book of becoming, of temporal or bodily exchange such that saying, "Mrs. Richardson raises a glass," or, "Haywood," again and again, or, "Dear Mrs. Baxter," "Dear Mrs. Barbauld," or, "the book in my hands says," or, "I go too far in one direction and then I turn around" was also to say, "each moment corresponds to a different room" or "We all agreed to this" or "I almost interview myself and experience my whole life story" or "Today in History." "So I decide to count the number of steps from our front door to the first duck standing upright on the half-frozen pond in the park," I began to want to say about many things. I began to want to replace my language for explaining what I've seen with the sentences of this book because these sentences said the thing I wanted to say, getting at all the elusive twists and flatnesses and velocities. You wanted the objects of your world to show your stuttering through, to open up your paths from the "I" to the verb, make everything a house, a bird, some kind of myopic sighting, some glimpse into another world, and you wanted to add a hum where there was too much silence and utter silence where there was noise and always some in-between gestures that made it impossible to really know which was which, and as Dutton warns us, "It takes a long time, maybe eighty-five years."

RENEE GLADMAN

ACKNOWLEDGMENTS

Thank you to the editors who first published sections of *SPRAWL* in *BOMB, Bombay Gin, The Brooklyn Rail, The Collagist, CutBank, Design Observer, Harper's, interbirth, jubilat, Shiny, Sleepingfish, Tarpaulin Sky,* and *Where We Live Now: An Annotated Reader.* Warmhearted thanks to Lisa Pearson at Siglio Press for publishing *SPRAWL* in 2010. Warmhearted thanks to Heidi Broadhead and everyone at Wave Books for giving this book new life in 2018.

Laura Letinsky's still-life photographs, in *Laura Letinsky: Hardly More Than Ever: Photographs 1997–2004* (The Renaissance Society at the University of Chicago, 2004), were instrumental to the imagining of this book.

The following writers and their works unknowingly provided words and ideas for use in the writing of *SPRAWL*: Henry David Thoreau in *Walden*; Georges Perec in *Species of Spaces and Other Pieces*; Lyn Hejinian in "Two Stein Talks" and "The Rejection of Closure"; Hanneke Grootenboer in "The Posthumous Lives of Leftovers: Photographs by Laura Letinsky"; Ludwig Wittgenstein in *Philosophical Investigations*; Carla

Harryman in "How I Wrote *Gardener of Stars*, a Novel"; Norbert Schneider in *Still Life: Still Life Painting in the Early Modern Period*; Alison J. Clarke in "Tupperware: Suburbia, sociality and mass consumption"; Nan Freeman in "Tom Wesselmann: Still-Life Painting and American Culture, circa 1962"; Virginia Woolf in *Moments of Being*; Alan Wearne in *The Nightmarkets*; Renee Gladman in *The Activist* and "The Person in the World"; Petra Ten-Doesschate Chu in "Emblems for a Modern Age: Vincent van Gogh's Still Lifes and the Nineteenth-Century Vignette Tradition"; Charlotte Brontë in *Villette*; John Cheever in *The Journals of John Cheever*; Vicky Lebeau in "The Worst of All Possible Worlds?"; William James in *The Principles of Psychology*; Nancy G. Duncan and James S. Duncan in "Deep Suburban Irony"; John Berger in *Ways of Seeing*; Thomas Hobbes in *Leviathan*; Ian Watt in *The Rise of the Novel*; Robert Messia in "Lawns as Artifacts: The Evolution of Social and Environmental Implications of Suburban Residential Land Use"; Ralph Waldo Emerson in "Compensation"; Rikki Ducornet in *The Monstrous and the Marvelous*; Milton Curry in "Racial Critique of Public Housing Redevelopment Strategies"; Pamela Lu in *Pamela: A Novel*; Gertrude Stein in "The Winner Loses: A Picture of Occupied France" and *The Autobiography of Alice B. Toklas*; John Archer in "Colonial Suburbs in South Asia, 1700– 1850, and the Spaces of Modernity"; Amanda Rees in "New Urbanism: Visionary Landscapes in the Twenty-First Century"; Josh Protas in "The Straw That Broke the Camel's Back: Preservation of an Urban Mountain

Landscape"; Brian Kiteley in *The 3 A.M. Epiphany*; John Hartley in "The Sexualization of Suburbia"; Lynn Spigel in "From Theatre to Space Ship: Metaphors of suburban domesticity in postwar America"; Lydia Davis in "Form as Response to Doubt"; Michele Byers in "Waiting at the Gate: The New, Postmodern Promised Lands"; Robert Urquhart in *Ordinary Choices: Individuals, Incommensurability, and Democracy*; Laura (Riding) Jackson in *Anarchism Is Not Enough*; James Howard Kunstler in *Home from Nowhere: Remaking Our Everyday World for the 21st Century*; Northrop Frye in *The Modern Century*; Roland Barthes in "The World as Object"; Bhanu Kapil in *Incubation: A Space for Monsters*; Steve Featherstone in "The Line Is Hot: A history of the machine gun, shot"; Diane Williams in *Romancer Erector*; Reindert Falkenburg in "Matters of Taste: Pieter Aertsen's Market Scenes, Eating Habits, and Pictorial Rhetoric in the Sixteenth Century"; Wilton & Wilton in *Pictorial Encyclopedia of Modern Cake Decorating*.

This book was and is for Marty.